A Flower Blooms on Charlotte Street

The Adventures of Ociee Nash

See the film based on this book.
A film by CineVita Productions, starring Keith Carradine, Mare
Winningham, and, introducing, Skyler Day, with Tom Key and
Ty Pennington.

A Flying Zebras film.

Screenplay by Amy and Kristen McGary.
Directed by Kristen McGary.
Produced by Amy McGary.
Music by Van Dyke Parks
Film editor, Amy Carey Linton
Production Designer, Margaret Hungerford
Director of Photography, Brian Gunter
Producer, Derek Kavanaugh
Associate Producer, Stephen Dirkes
Costume Designer, Susan E. Mickey
Casting Director, Shirley Fulton Crumley

Visit the website at

www.ociee.com

A Flower Blooms on Charlotte Street

With all happy wishes to Summer's daddy —

A Novel

We love your daughter!

by

Milam McGraw Propst

Milam McGraw Propst

Mercer University Press

Macon, Georgia

July 4, 2010

ISBN 0-86554-960-5
MUP/P307

03 02 01 00 99   5 4 3 2 1

Originally published in 1999
in hardcover by Mercer University Press

∞The paper used in this publication meets the
minimum requirements of American National
Standard for Information Sciences — Permanence of
Paper for Printed Library Materials, ANSI Z39.48-
1984.

All photographs used by courtesy of CineVita Production

Library of Congress Cataloging-in-Publication Data

Propst, Milam McGraw.
A flower blooms on Charlotte Street: a novel /
by Milam McGraw Propst — 1st ed.
p. vi + 171
ISBN 0-86554-960-5 (alk. paper)
I. Title.
PS3566.R67F58   1998
813'.54 — dc21   98-46966
CIP

Acknowledgments

I watch award shows with fervor. Always have, always will. Of particular interest to me are the winners' speeches. It is now obvious just how difficult it is for those famous folks to encapsulate years of gratitude into a few seconds of dialogue.

That said, here's my own list. Thank you Marc Jolley of Mercer University Press for giving Ociee life following an extended period of gestation. Thank you, Carol Lee Lorenzo, author and instructor, along with Charles Scarritt of the University of Alabama, and Sister Thomas Margaret of St. Pius High School—thank you three for teaching me to write.

Thank you Pam, Jackie and Betty, Mary, Dannie, Janelle, Marilynn, Betty Ann, Laura, Jody, and Dorothy for encouraging me in my work. Thank you to my husband Jamey for cooking your wonderful meals and for being responsible, in general, while I was lost in rural Mississippi in 1898. Thank you to our parents who provided the role models for the assortment of the characters who people the pages of Ociee's story.

And thank you to our precious children, Amanda, William, and Jay, for contributing bits and pieces of your own childhoods to give new voices to your great-grandmother and her siblings.

I dedicate this book to my B, who is, to everyone else, Ociee.
To me, she is B, my cherished grandmother.

Part One

Ociee and Ben
(Courtesy of CineVita Productions)

Ociee and her dog.
(Courtesy of CineVita Productions)

Ociee and the Gypsy.
(Courtesy of CineVita Productions)

1

"Where are you, Ociee?" shouted Ben as the kitchen door slammed loud behind him. "You gotta see, you just gotta see!" My brother's blond curls dripped wet from running hard. Ben's gray green eyes wide, he sputtered out the words, "It's a real gypsy, Ociee! And he's set up his camp down by Miller's Creek. Come on, quit fooling with those dern beans, girl. Come on, aren't you hearing me?"

I tossed the handful I'd been stringing back in Mama's blue bean bowl. Annoyed as much as curious I said, "What's this commotion about a gypsy, Ben Nash?" At that time, all I knew about gypsies was exactly what folks said. I heard that they were strange, strange, *and dangerous*. What's more, I believed we were smart enough to leave them be. I picked up a bean and shook it at him saying, "Can't you see I'm busy getting supper ready?"

"Gracious sakes, Ociee," he panted, "Supper's every night, the gypsy is right now!"

There was no saying "no" once my brother got going on anything. I don't know why I tried that time either. I hardly got my apron off when he pulled me from my chair and pushed me out the kitchen door.

Ben was talking fast as lightning. "Ociee, I was up on the top of the rise watching as that old gypsy stopped to give his horse a drink from the creek. He looked around real careful, kind of like he was making sure no one saw him. Then he said some foreign stuff to the horse. Next thing I knew, he was settling in and starting a campfire. I came straight home to get you."

I couldn't argue. Ben was right. Imagine, a really and true gypsy was camped near our farm. We had to watch what he was doing. Surely Papa would understand why I had to go with Ben.

3

He wouldn't worry, not for a minute. Papa would say, "Ociee, go on, see for yourself." Well, maybe he would.

We raced like wild ponies straight toward Miller's Creek. Through the apple orchard, up the clay bank, around the old Indian burial ground, my heart pounded. Thoughts of gypsies pushed me faster than I had ever run before. We reached the crest of the hill.

"Stop!" Ben threw his arm back across my chest. Putting his finger to his lips, he said, "Shhh! See! What'd I tell you? There it is, an honest to gosh gypsy wagon." His chest puffed out with pride.

"Gracious, Ben, I never saw anything like it, look, oh just look at that." I breathed in the scene.

The gypsy didn't appear to be there, so we decided to creep closer to take a better look. Easing downhill toward the creek bank, we gripped each other's hands as much for courage as to balance ourselves.

I was excited, scared, but mostly, proud that Ben had asked me to go with him.

We made our way across the creek struggling on its water-slick rocks. We approached the camp like two wary deer in search for food.

"Easy," urged Ben.

"Easy, yourself, Ben Nash. I'm just fine," I frowned at him. What I wanted him to notice was how brave I was acting.

The gypsy wagon loomed much larger as we got close to it. "Ben, it's tall as our barn!" I exclaimed. That August afternoon in 1898, our barn suddenly seemed farther away than the country mile we had just run. That afternoon, Marshall County, Mississippi, our home, was as far away to me as Papa's favorite star.

Inquisitive more than courageous, we inched ever closer. The side of the wagon we could see was the rich blue of a sky in autumn. In the center, sunshine sparkled on a gold border which outlined the fancy painting of odd-shaped trees and extraordinary birds that surely never nested anywhere near Mississippi.

The best part was the beautiful lady in the center of the picture. She was olive-skinned with crystal blue eyes. Her gold earrings glistened through her long curly brown hair. She wore a bright purple veil and her shoulders were draped in a deep red shawl with black tassels. Other people were painted far back almost as if they were walking toward us from a deeper place hidden inside the wagon.

I felt like I was under a magic spell. "Oh Ben, it's so pretty. Look at the blue and gold sky. It makes me think of the painting on the back wall in Sunday School class. Why, it looks like Heaven."

"The pretty lady makes me think of Mama," he said.

"Does she look like Mama to you?"

Mama had been dead almost a year, but it was like the sad just kept hanging on to us all: to Ben, to Papa, to our big brother Fred, and to me. Sometimes I'd open my eyes in the early morning. I'd feel happy just for an instant only to be jolted awake by the dreadful memory of Mama lying there in that cold pine box in the front of church.

I studied the painting on the gypsy wagon.

I couldn't say whether the lady really looked like Mama or not. The fact was I had a hard time remembering exactly how Mama looked. I squeezed my eyes shut to try to clear my memory's blurred picture of Mama's joyful face. Like always, the image faded until it was gone.

Ben kept right on talking. "I'll bet those are angels in the way back part of the picture," he said setting his jaw. He squinted hard looking for details in the painted faces.

A sudden burst of wind shattered my gentle daydream. Even though it was hot summertime, a horrible chill seized me. A noise came from inside the wagon. The hairs on my arm stood straight. A second sound. I couldn't move for fear.

BAAM! Crash!

The door of the gypsy wagon flew open. I heard an ominous roar. The enormous man thundered out from inside his wagon. The earth rumbled as he stomped down the trembling wood steps. His greasy curls were tied back in a red bandanna, a single gold earring swung back and forth in a hole stretched long from time. The gypsy spat with the breath of a fiery dragon and bellowed, "You keeds, get away from here, or I weel eat you for my supper."

"Run for home, Ociee!" shouted Ben.

My eyes riveted on the monster man, yet somehow my feet obeyed my brother's voice. We took off and ran straight through the creek. No slippery rocks would trap us. Wet shoes wouldn't matter because we were running for our very lives. I chanced to look back. Putting his massive hands on his brown belted hips, the gypsy man reared back his head and laughed. His laugh welled up from way down inside his big belly.

The sound echoed through the valley way past the Indian mound. We raced for the safety of home. I wondered if the spirits of those long-dead Indians shuddered in their graves at the sound of his deep roaring bellow.

I stumbled and fell over a broken tree limb. I landed on my arm. My elbow was bleeding, but I wasn't about to cry.

Ben doubled back to help me up. "Are you okay?"

"'Course, I am, Ben. Let's go."

"Hurry then," he shouted.

"Oh, Ben, I hope Papa's home."

"Me, too, Ociee. Or, at least, Fred."

We made it through the orchard. No gypsy followed. Our farm was mercifully in sight. Closer and closer we got to the shelter of home. Then, thank the good Lord, I spotted Fred coming in from the pasture. I knew we'd be safe with him in sight. We charged through the chicken yard. "Out of my way, Hector, you old rooster." Dirt dusted up, chickens scattered.

Up the steps, we charged across the porch and into our house. Ben slammed the door behind us and held it tight with his whole body. We were panting our lungs out. Caked with dirty sweat, grass, leaves and water, I took a deep, deep breath and collapsed at the kitchen table.

Fred raced up onto the porch. As he kicked the rail to get mud clods off his work boots, he hollered, "What in the world have you two been up to now? I just saw chickens flying every which away."

I ran outside into my brother's huge arms. Ben charged up behind me and grabbed Fred's shoulders shouting, "A gypsy, Fred, a gypsy chased me and Ociee all the way home."

My hands on Fred's cheeks, I turned his head toward me and screamed, "He must be ten feet tall."

Fred listened.

"And sure as sunshine, he breathed fire right on us." I showed my elbow. "See, this is my burned place."

"Ociee, that's where you fell." Ben interrupted.

"After he breathed that fire on me." I insisted.

Fred hung on every word. Even though he had never seen a gypsy close up, he knew a lot about most things and that, of course, included gypsies.

"Fred, he had a wagon tall as our barn," I tried to tell, but, of course, Ben corrected me, "Two barns, at least, Ociee."

Our big brother gently eased both of us back inside and asked, "Do you know why gypsies have such tall wagons?"

Wide-eyed, we shook our heads no.

Scratching his chin, Fred explained, "That's so they can keep farm children locked up in the top of the wagons and cook 'em in big pots whenever they get hungry for supper!"

With that, he bit Ben on his neck.

Ben jumped sky high.

I screamed at the top of my lungs.

Fred gathered us up into his strong arms and the three of us rolled around on the kitchen's cool wood floor.

Ben raised up on his elbows, "Fred, you gotta go back with us. You just gotta see." he pleaded.

"Tonight, when it's good and dark?" suggested Fred.

"Well, maybe in the morning instead," Ben said. "So we can see his camp site better."

"Oh, so we can *see* better?" Fred was grinning.

"Let's ask Papa to go, too," I suggested. "Papa's braver than that old gypsy. With Papa and Fred, we wouldn't ever worry about being any gypsy's supper. Supper! I clean forgot all about supper."

2

We all pitched in to fix our evening meal. Fred started a fire in the wood stove. I finished stringing the beans and buttered the leftover breakfast biscuits for toasting. Ben started to set the table, but, as usual, he found it necessary to complain, "A gypsy-chasing boy shouldn't have to do kitchen work. It's not right."

Fred cocked his head and said, "Who chased who, Ben?"

"Well, I did have to see about Ociee," Ben said.

"Is that how come you got across the creek long before me, Ben? You had *to see about Ociee?*"

I had him good, but lucky for Ben, he didn't have to answer because I spotted Papa's wagon coming up the road. With the excitement of Papa coming in, any squabbles always came to a halt. Papa's homecoming was the best part of every day for us Nashes.

"Papa's coming," I said running outside. Ben jumped over the porch rail to beat me to him.

"I found a gypsy, Papa! He chased me and Ociee all the way home," Ben was hollering out the story.

I shouted, "Fred said we were lucky he didn't eat us there on the spot. Raw."

Ben said, "Papa, he ran hard. But we got away."

"And Papa, he growled," I added. "That's when I saw his fangs."

Papa jumped down and hugged us tight. "Lord help us. What are the two of you doing chasing after a stranger like that?" He put his mighty sunburned arms around Ben and me. With a look of worry in his eyes, Papa walked us inside and sat down to listen about our adventure.

We were telling him where the camp was set up when, all of a sudden, I touched my neck.

"Mama's locket," I shrieked. "Mama's locket is gone!"

"Oh no, Ociee," moaned Papa.

In my panic, I tried to think. "I put it on this morning, like always."

Papa told the boys and me to spread out to search. "That locket is hiding just waiting to be found," said Papa. "Let's see who will be the first to see it."

My heart ached as I began to look. How well I remembered the day it was given to me. We had just returned from the church, from Mama's funeral service. All those people, the neighbors, the community had come to our house. The farmers dressed in dark suits, their hard weathered hands reached to embrace me. Their hands looked out of place coming from starched white cuffs instead of the colorful plaid sleeves that usually reached to give me a taste of cane sugar. The ladies weren't wearing bright calico prints. They wore instead the black, the dreary black of mourning. The long black dresses flowed like a river of black. How I wished the dank, dark river would flow through my house and all the way out to the Gulf of Mexico.

I stood silently in the corner of our parlor. One of the black skirts drifted toward me. It said, "Oh, poor little motherless child." The skirt enveloped me. I bolted and tried to run outside. I wanted to disappear.

Another skirt rushed in my path. It said, "Precious child, where are you going?" It spoke with a familiar voice. Emerging from my self-imposed mist, I recognized my Aunt Mamie, Papa's sister.

"Oh, Aunt Mamie, I hate this so much. I hate all the ugly clothes and awful big black hats. Where is my Mama? I want her. Aunt Mamie, I don't want all this noise in our house."

She hugged me close. It wasn't with the hug of people feeling sorry for me. It was the hug of a person to whom I belonged. We walked out the front parlor door and into the yard. I was crying so hard my eyes couldn't see where we were going. Aunt Mamie dabbed away my tears with her lace hankie. "There, there, little girls are supposed to cry when they are sad," she said. "It's the way you wash away the hurt inside."

She walked me toward Mama's yellow rose bush. Aunt Mamie took her arm from around me, reached up and carefully removed two blossoms. One she put in the band of her hat and the second she put through the button hole of my dress. She said, "I know your Mama wouldn't like all this black either, Ociee. She would choose these bright colors to decorate the both of us."

We went back inside and the next time I got sad with the black, I sniffed my rose and felt its warm color. That was the night that Papa and Aunt Mamie had given me Mama's locket.

Now it was lost. I vowed to find it. The locket was really all I had of Mama that was just mine alone. I went to look in my room. I searched my washstand, the bed, on, under, and all around it, on the floor, all around the doors, the windows, in my trunk. I already had the sick and sad feeling Mama's locket was somewhere between home and Miller's Creek. Yet, I continued to search.

In a way, Mama's locket belonged to the whole family even though Papa and Aunt Mamie had chosen to give it to me. Lost, lost, lost. It was like losing part of Mama all over again.

My brothers combed the dirt yard and down toward and around the barn, the coops, the smokehouse, and shed. Papa looked about the outside of the house and around the porch and down into the cellar.

Inside, I kept looking in the same spots over and over and over again. Discouraged, I wandered into the parlor and walked toward Papa's desk. He kept his most important things in there, and we children weren't allowed to go in the drawers. "Papa," I leaned out the window and asked, "may I look in your desk?"

"Here I come, Ociee. It's worth our taking a look together."

That was just like Papa. He was always helping us and everyone else with anything we asked. I prayed that Mama swooped up the locket with her angel's wings and carefully placed it in Papa's drawer for us to find.

Together, Papa and I started to dig. There was no miracle.

"Papa," I pleaded, "Show me your college papers one more time."

"Ociee dear, don't you ever tire of seeing that ancient history?" he sighed. I think he was just as glad to get both our minds off the lost locket, if only for awhile. "Well, let's see, here's the story about the wagon train, oh, and my poems from English, business notes. Haven't looked at this in some time, my letter of acceptance. Ancient history it is! But, I suppose your old father was smart enough to spend some time at the University of North Carolina."

"And smart enough to be the very best farmer in the whole state of Mississippi," I bragged.

"That, my daughter, remains to be seen. My heart isn't as sure about this great venture of ours now that your Mama's not at my side." He got real quiet.

Then to break the sorrow, Papa clasped his hands together, looked at me and said, "Listen to me being glum when I have so much to cherish. I have you three, our land, this home. Here, give your Papa hug. I *am* a fortunate man."

Together, we continued to search the desk. Records, receipts, some photos. All we were accomplishing was not finding the locket and seeing things with Mama's handwriting. Papa said it wasn't as sorrowful as it was finding more treasures. To me, however, Mama's writing only made things worse.

Papa must have understood, "I'm too hungry to hunt just now. What do you say we call the boys in and feed this bunch of Nashes?"

I sort of agreed. But I wasn't the least bit hungry.

True to his spirit, Papa tried to make things seem better than they actually were. "I'm sure we'll soon find it, Ociee. But it's getting late now. Don't you worry just yet, that locket will find it's way back to you."

Papa was right about most things, but that time it seemed more like he was saying what we all needed to hear.

Ben stomped into the kitchen, "No luck yet, Ociee, but I'll look for it all over Marshall County if I have to. I'll get Mama's locket back for you."

Behind him came Fred saying, "It won't be lost for long, Ociee." They were George Nash's sons all right. I acted like I believed them all, but I didn't.

Papa kicked off his boots and looked into the bubbling bean pot. Taking a big sniff, he said, "Mmm, something smells mighty good, I always perk up once I have a full stomach. Let's settle down and have some supper."

It was Wednesday, Ben's turn to say the blessing.

"Lord, make us thankful. Papa, do you suppose he says grace?"

"He who, son?"

"The gypsy, Papa."

Fred jumped in, "Yes, Ben, tonight that man will likely pray, 'Thank you, Lord, for that tasty farm boy I nearly caught today. I can't wait for him to come back by here, amen.'"

"Oh, Papa," I shrieked. Ben just stared mouth agape.

"Fred is teasing you both. He probably heard crazy stories like that when he was little."

Ben stood up, then raring back his shoulders, he poked his nose way up and shouted, "Little? Look at how tall I am."

Papa said, "Sit yourself down, Ben. You are both getting too grown up for me. You're growing as fast as honeysuckle vines. In fact, you and Ociee are so big I believe right now is a fine time to learn something new about human nature."

"Yes, sir," said Ben. He shuffled in his seat. He didn't always enjoy Papa's teaching. Ben usually wiggled too much for learning things.

"Yes, sir," I echoed, but all I was really thinking about was Mama's locket lost out there in the almost dark.

Papa said, "Folks tend to tell tales so much they become true. Ben, I believe that gypsy means no harm to any one."

"Papa, you didn't see his mean eyes." Ben insisted.

"Ben, Ben, calm yourself. He's not what you're accustomed to, so you are letting yourself imagine all kinds of craziness. Gracious sakes, I should be worried about *his* safety, now that Ben Nash is after him!"

We laughed, but Ben sat there and made a face.

"Ben, now promise me you won't be bothering that man. Promise me, son." Papa would use 'son' when he was serious.

"I promise," Ben sighed. He was trying hard not to wiggle. I could tell.

I decided it was a good time to tell Papa about the painting. I said, "Papa, Fred, the gypsy's wagon was decorated with pretty pictures like the ones in Sunday School. There was the most beautiful lady in a painting. She had a veil and gold jewelry and long pretty hair." I tossed back my head to show off my own curls. "There were faraway birds and a blue sky filled with clouds and angels. We thought it was Heaven."

"Not me," said Ben. "I didn't."

"You did too think it was Heaven, Ben, remember you were looking for Mama in the picture," I said.

"Well, all right, maybe I did."

Papa smiled his sad remembering smile like always when folks talked about Mama. Then, like he also tended to do, he completely changed what we were talking about. He jumped up and said, "Children, I nearly forgot! Miss May fixed us a pie. It's in the wagon unless, of course, Gray Dog ate it."

With that, Ben yelled, "Last one to Papa's wagon gets the little piece." We charged outside. Ben beat me to it.

Papa reached down under the wagon seat and pulled out the prize. He rolled back the gingham cloth and showed us the still warm crust stuffed full of Miss May's best peaches. His eyes meeting ours one by one, he said, "Now, children, take a whiff."

"Mmm," I closed my eyes and said, "Peaches, butter, crusty sugar."

He pointed to Gray Dog, dead asleep and snoring under the pine tree. "Too bad fellow, I'm sorry the pie smell didn't quite drift your way. Lucky for us people, I'd say."

Fred said, "Let's take it inside. How about we cut it into four great big equal-size pieces?"

"Wait! I got here first," objected Ben.

Papa looked at Ben.

"That will be four *equal* pieces," said Papa.

While Papa served the pie, I put our supper dishes to soak in thick, soapy water. Fred hurried outside to see to Papa's mare, Maude. Ben went to help.

We soon gathered back at the table and ate every bite of that pie. "This one was the best Miss May ever made," said Papa. Of course, that's what we traditionally said about anything that lady would bake for us.

Then Papa said, "Fred, you and Ben finish for us. Ociee, you and I are going to sit on the front porch."

Fred and Papa kind of eyeballed one another, but I didn't think much about it until later.

3

Papa took my hand and we walked out of the kitchen. Ben gave me a mean-eyed look and stuck out his tongue. I just tossed my curls and prissed on out. We crossed through the dining room and down the hall straight through the parlor by Mama's picture.

"Papa, why isn't Mama smiling in her picture?"

"Ociee, I don't know. I think your Mama thought it was stylish to pose that way." His voice trailed off, "Truthfully, I have wondered if she had a forewarning the good Lord was planning to take her to be with Him. As much as she dreamed of being with the angels, she would have been troubled about leaving all of us."

"Papa, promise *you* won't you get one of those warnings, promise! We just couldn't bear it."

"Your Papa is just fine, I do promise. Don't you worry yourself about such a thing."

I looked up at Mama's face. Papa squeezed my hand.

The front door shut behind us. We sat ourselves on the porch swing. Even stretching long, my feet couldn't touch the wooden floor of the porch so I let Papa do the swinging.

The air stirred and cooled our hot, sticky faces. My hair blew back from my face. He twisted one of my curls around his finger.

We were quiet as we swung back and forth in the night air. "What am I to do with you, my Ociee? Here you are the prettiest thing I ever saw, yet you spend your days either all by yourself in our house or running with Ben around Marshall County. And you're wearing boy's dungarees to boot."

"Oh, Papa, don't be teasing me, I'm not so pretty. Am I?"

"Indeed you are, Miss Ociee."

I liked to sit with Papa.

We sat on the porch for a long time listening to the crickets chirp. The stars dotted the sky and the summer moon floated in and out of soft gray clouds.

I heard Ben arguing way back through the kitchen window, "Fred, I did the dishes last night. It's Ociee's turn to do the supper chores." Mostly, he wanted to come outside and see what we were doing. Ben and Fred, and me, too, loved those special talks by ourselves with Papa. This was one of my turns. Ben was jealous, plain to see.

Papa spoke. "Ociee, it's just not right how you live here on the farm with all us men folk. It's more like you are a tough little boy rather than the frilly girl you would be with a Mama around."

"Mama wasn't all frilly, Papa." I said. "She was funny, too."

Papa had agreed with me. "Ociee, do you remember the time you all had the soap suds fight? There she was washing shirts in the metal tub out back when Gray Dog came and jumped right in," Papa laughed. "Mama tried to turn that into a bath for Gray and he didn't like that one bit. Leaped out, he did just yelping. I was coming in for lunch about that time. There was the dog, covered in soap and Mama running after him. Ben came running, he slid and tumbled down. Mama ran back to see if Ben was hurt. Old soapy Gray Dog turned and charged back after the two of them. Then there you came, Ociee. You didn't want to miss out. You jumped off the porch to be in on the soap fight, too. Maybe, just maybe, I got in on it, too."

"Papa, I remember, you were a BIG part of that soap fight!" I giggled.

"Poor Gray Dog, he never was much for a bath, especially after that," said Papa. "I'm afraid he gets about as clean as he's going to paddling around in our pond."

"Frilly ladies wouldn't play with dogs in wash tubs, would they, Papa?"

"Ociee, your Mama was a little bit of all ladies. She could be funny just like when she was playing with you children. Then she could be prim and proper, you remember, like putting all

17

her lace doilies around in the parlor and pouring tea for neighbors when they came by for a visit."

"And stylish, Papa, like posing real serious like for her portrait?" I added.

"Yes, and, pretty. Why Ociee, that's where you get your prettiness. You surely don't look like your old Papa."

I scrooched down and snuggled up next to him. "You are too handsome, Papa." I said.

We sat there for a bit. All at once, I said, "Papa, I'll be ten in November, I'll be more like a girl when I'm ten. I could fix tea for the neighbors."

Papa smiled.

"Right now Ben and I have so much fun. He wouldn't have fun with a regular girl. Like today when he came and got me to see that gypsy. He wouldn't have wanted a prissy old girl along. I was so brave, you know. Why, I didn't even cry when I fell."

"You are one brave girl," Papa laughed. "But that's what I'm talking about. I wish you hadn't fallen then. I wish you were always safe and watched out for like girls in Abbeville."

"I watch out for me, Papa."

"I know, Ociee, I know." He gave my elbow a kiss just exactly where it hurt.

We kept swinging. The crickets chirped.

"Papa," shouted Fred, "I'm going to feed the pigs. I've got grouchy britches with me, *maybe*, he'll be some help."

"Fred, stop picking on me," Ben yelled as they walked toward the pig pen.

Papa breathed in. "Ociee, your Aunt Mamie is always writing to me about how much she loves you and the boys." said Papa. "It's a shame that she's so far away that she can't spend near enough time with us. North Carolina is too far away from Mississippi—just so far very far away." His voice drifted again.

I thought about how much better Aunt Mamie made things seem. I thought about the yellow rose bush. It was blooming again. I thought about the locket. I looked at Papa and said, "Mama's locket, oh Papa, I feel lonely without it on my neck."

Papa said, "Shhhh, please don't worry. We will find it, I promise you that."

"That's two promises tonight, Papa. I'll try to believe."

He replied with a tight snuggle.

Maybe just to change my sad thinking, I asked, "Papa, does Aunt Mamie still sew dresses for ladies in North Carolina?"

"That she does, real pretty ones. We all ought to be very proud of her."

"I am. But, Papa, I want to do something so's to make you proud of me."

"Why, Ociee, you do every day, just by being my daughter. I enjoy walking down the street with you by my side. And, little lady, when I spot you coming across the field sometimes, I tell you I grow taller right then and there. Why, I must be nearly six feet tall because of all that pride you send my way."

"Oh, Papa, you're teasing me again."

"Maybe a little, but it's teasing about something true."

"Papa, do you think I look anything like Aunt Mamie?"

"Well, Ociee, I suppose you do at that. You are a nice combination of Aunt Mamie and your Mama. You seem to have Mamie's coloring with your Mama's eyes, her mouth, her expression."

That was nice to know.

We swung back and forth.

Papa continued, "You do understand that Mamie and us are close just like you and the boys because we are family. Even though we don't see each other, there is a real closeness between Aunt Mamie, all the way in Asheville and our family here in Mississippi. As much as you love your brothers this evening, you will discover that you will love each other even more when you get grown."

"More, I hope," I giggled.

"Yes, even more," he agreed, "And, remember, that doesn't change even if you are far away from each other."

I tried to imagine me or Fred or even Ben getting old, old like Papa and Aunt Mamie.

19

Papa spoke again, "Ociee, when your Mama and I were first married we lived with Mamie while we saved to buy our farm. We lived in the house where she lives today. See, right here on this envelope," he said as he showed me, "66 Charlotte Street, Asheville, North Carolina."

"Did you know Mama was very uneasy about saying good-bye to those North Carolina mountains that she loved so dearly? Only because I pleaded with her, was she willing to come. She had been so happy in Asheville, but she knew I yearned so to try my hand with this farm. Part of me feels bad about it. She was a brave, strong woman, your Mama."

"Papa, she must have loved you more than she loved any mountains," I suggested.

"Yes, Ociee, I know she did, she did that."

All at once, the hum of the chirping and the squeak of the swing was interrupted by a loud commotion.

"Dag nabit," Ben shouted, "Stupid pig! What did you go and move for? Made me slip. You dumb pig."

Papa and I stopped swinging and ran toward the barn.

"Stupid pig?" Fred was laughing uncontrollably. "More like stupid boy!"

Fred reached to fish Ben from the pig pen. His arms outstretched, Fred chuckled, "I can't see anything but mud and eyes and teeth."

Sqursh-sploop! Just as we got to the pen, Fred yanked Ben out of the sticky, gooey Mississippi mud. Papa and I had our arms around each other as we watched the show. We laughed so hard we had to hold one another up.

Ben was wild with the indignity of his situation. He was spitting and kicking as he fought to shake off the nasty brown gunk.

Papa said, "Let's get this mud stack to the well and pour a few buckets of water over it. Fred, Ociee, do you suppose we'll find a boy in this muddy goo? Or when it's washed away, will we come upon one angry little pig?"

"A boy, that's what!" gurgled Ben.

Papa pointed him toward the well.

I asked Fred if Ben was hurt.

"Just his pride, Ociee, just his pride." laughed Fred.

Ben heard and shouted back to us, "My pride's fine, it's my dern bottom I hit." He wouldn't have let himself laugh for all candy in Mississippi.

Fred winked at me.

After a bucket shower and a serious soap scrubbing, Ben stomped back inside our house to towel dry his hair.

I started around the house but stopped beside the porch when I heard a different tone in Fred's voice. I listened. I overheard him ask Papa if he had shared Aunt Mamie's letter with me as yet. Papa spoke sort of low, "I'm afraid we got a bit distracted just now."

Fred replied, "I'm sorry, Papa. Reckon we should have been more careful."

Papa continued, "No, son, actually, I'm fighting myself to get those words out. Besides, there's time, Fred, there's still a little time."

4

I woke up the next morning when our fine loud rooster called to me. "Cock-a-doodle-Ociee. Cock-a-doodle-do." The sun was on its way up and my feet hit the floor ready for a summer morning.

I was glad to find Papa already in the kitchen with bacon sizzling in the cast iron skillet. Grits were popping in the big pot.

"Good morning, Papa."

"Good morning, Ociee, did you hear your cockadoodle call?"

"Sure did. How come Hector doesn't say, 'Cock-a-doodle-Ben or Cock-a-doodle-Fred?'" I asked.

"That's because he's a lady's man. How do you want your eggs this fine morning, Miss Ociee?" said Papa.

"Why, Papa, fried with the yellows up so I can pop them with my fork, please."

Papa told me to set the table. I got out our green plates and the yellow checked napkins, four places with Papa at the head. Glasses for Ben's milk and mine, a jar of blackberry jelly, butter, coffee cups for Papa and Fred.

"Papa, should I drink coffee after my next birthday?"

Papa suggested, "No, I think you should try a half cup this very morning. We'll pour in lots of cream and sugar. I warn you. Coffee smells a whole lot better than it tastes until you get accustomed to its flavor."

"Maybe I'll just wait 'til I'm ten for coffee drinking." I put only two cups out, one for Papa and one for Fred. Ben and I would have milk.

"The boys are out in the barn already," Papa said.

I stepped out on the back porch. It had rained a little during the night and everything had taken on the smell of clean. The sun was beginning to toast our farm with the morning warm.

Maude, Gray Dog and the cows and chickens were joining the rooster making their hungry morning neighs, woofs, clucks and moos. Pig grunts made me giggle thinking about Ben last night.

I heard the sounds of the day's chores, of buckets clanking and of feed being poured, and, naturally, I could hear Ben's chattering. He sounded like one of our clucking chickens.

Rain droplets sparkled from the leaves of Mama's bushes. Little puddles shined all around the dirt yard like jewels. With a start, I thought about Mama's locket. It was almost as bad as remembering Mama's death. The rain likely washed it far from our looking. I wrapped my arms around close and wished it was still safe on my neck. "It may be gone, Ociee Nash," I told me, "best get used to the idea." But I also told myself to keep on looking for it.

I watched out across the fields where Papa and Fred and Papa's hired help would work to put in our fall crops. I spotted Fred with the cows.

"Papa, I see Rebecca." I shouted through the kitchen door. "My calf sure is getting big!"

"Growing up as fast as you are, I would say, Ociee."

"Oh, Papa, I'm not growing that fast," I said.

I had named Rebecca after Fred's sweetheart, but she never was too pleased about it. Rebecca, the person, lived in Abbeville. Besides Rebecca, Abbeville also had a post office, a hotel, eight stores, the railroad station, our school house, three churches and bunches of houses and offices where men conducted business. To Fred, Rebecca was the most important thing about Abbeville. He acted so foolish around her. It made Ben and me laugh. Once he kissed her and we saw. Ben pretended to vomit.

Rebecca was a town girl, which explained why she didn't understand anything about calves. Rightfully, she should have been flattered my calf was named for her. But she wasn't.

I recalled the time when Fred and I were out in the barn with my calf. I told Fred that my Rebecca was prettier than his Rebecca. He threw hay all over me and chased me. He knew I was right.

"Come on in here, girl," said Papa.

I went inside and watched Papa. He hummed as he stood over the stove. "Papa, how come your eggs always taste better than the ones that I fix?"

"Must be the way I hold this old fork, Ociee," he said, his eyes sparkling. He began to twist the fork around his ear, then circled his entire head and on down into the frying pan. "Now, if you please, madam, call the boys. "

Ben and Fred came running as soon as I rang the porch bell. Clang! Clang! We gathered again around the our table. Fred blessed our breakfast. "Lord make us thankful that we were able to find Ben in the pig pen last night, amen."

"Fred, forget that!" Ben turned red as his shirt.

"Who wants to go into town today?" Papa asked.

"I do, I do, I do," we three echoed. Fred would see Rebecca. Ben wanted to go any place, any time, and so did I, especially Abbeville. Of course, there would be work to do after we got home. But, none of us minded because our day was to be full of things far better than farm chores.

Papa had Fred hitch up Maude to the wagon. Ben fed the chickens. I finished up in the kitchen while Papa gathered his papers for business and picked up his money pouch. We were on our way.

I rode up front with Papa. Fred stretched out on the bed of the wagon likely to rest up for kissing with Rebecca. Ben sat in the back dangling his feet.

Papa whistled. "I like to take you into town with me and let folks see what fine children I have. We'd go even if I had no sugar or tools to buy. What a well blessed man I am this morning."

I felt proud riding with Papa. After we'd gone a mile or so, I asked him about the letter from Aunt Mamie that we never got around to reading on the porch.

At first, he didn't say anything, then he put his arm around me and pulled me close by his side. He said, "What I was trying to say to you last night was that Aunt Mamie and I, well, you know how we write back and forth?"

Maude trotted along in the bright morning sun. Papa handed me the reins for just a minute. He put his hand over mine as we both held tight to guide our wagon.

"I must have left Mamie's letter on the swing when we ran to pull Ben out of the mud."

A funny feeling came over me. Papa didn't usually hemyhaw so much about things.

He continued, "Mamie worries about us. Always has, but it's gotten worse since your Mama's been gone. Mamie makes suggestions about things. She writes how she loves us, and," he whispered, "especially, how she loves you."

"Can I tell the boys? Oh please, can I tell?"

Papa swallowed hard. I saw his whole neck tighten up. He didn't answer my question.

"You know that she misses you so much?" he started again.

"Papa! Is she coming back to see us?" I nearly jumped off the wagon seat.

Ben was singing in the back part of our wagon and must not have heard because he would have jumped over the seat to hear that news.

Fred had likely dozed off because he didn't say anything either.

"Is Aunt Mamie coming for a visit?"

Papa just stared ahead.

I was about to burst wide open, "Oh, say she is, please, say she is!"

Papa straightened his back, squeezed me close and slowed the mare. "Ociee, I just got to go on and tell you right now. Aunt Mamie wants me to send you to her in Asheville—Asheville, North Carolina."

5

I let go of the reins. Papa caught them. Frozen on that hot August day, my throat was tied in a knot just like Papa's. "Send me to Asheville, Papa?" I choked. "All the way to Asheville?"

"Yes, you're a big girl, Ociee." Papa uttered. "And you'll do fine, just fine. Aunt Mamie's been getting after me to send you. Oh, darling girl, this talk is coming out backwards and upside down."

"I love Aunt Mamie, but Papa, I've never been farther away than Abbeville. That was with you or Fred."

Papa kept trying to sound sure himself. He argued back, "You'll be plenty safe. I've seen all about that. Ociee, believe me, this will be the best thing. Mamie does so want you there with her."

It was like Papa was explaining to both of us. He was talking to himself as much as he was talking to me.

"Don't you need me, being that I am the *only* girl?" I said. "And whatever will Ben do without me? And Fred, too."

"Ociee, I've tried to figure on everything. I simply must put you first. Ben will be all right. He and Fred have each other.

"Papa, what about last night? You and Fred were talking about this then, weren't you? I saw you looking funny at each other."

"You don't miss a thing, do you, Ociee?"

"Not much, Papa."

"Yes, I've talked with him about it. At first, he argued with me about as much as you are. He finally gave in and said he would have to agree with the idea."

"Papa, what about you? I thought I helped you feel less sad. You know how much you like the pretty flowers around. Oh,

Papa, I will be more girlish, if you let me stay. I'll start making tea this very afternoon."

Papa reined in Maude. "Whoa, whoa, girl." Then he shook his head and cried real hard just like he did when Mama passed away.

I threw my arms around his neck. Fred stood up and made his way to the front of the wagon.

Ben's eyes were wild. He shouted, "Did somebody else die? What happened, what happened, Papa, Ociee? What is it, Fred?"

Our day that began with a happy wagon ride suddenly turned to misery. We climbed off our wagon and stood right in the middle of the road to Abbeville. Fred led Maude over to the side. We stood silent and waited for Papa to speak.

He slowly raised his head.

Another farmer was heading toward us on his horse. "Good morning, George, can I help you folks out? Something wrong with the wagon?"

Papa tipped his hat and motioned Mr. Hayes around our wagon. "Thanks, Hayes, we just stopped. That's all. Appreciate your worry."

Mr. Hayes went on.

Papa took off his straw hat, ran his fingers through his hair and wrinkled up the brim. "Ben, nobody has died and nobody is going to die this day, if I have any say." He cleared his throat. "This hasn't gone one bit like I planned."

Fred stood behind Ben and put his hands on his shoulders. Papa motioned us all over to stand under a big tree out of the hot sun.

"One way to explain this is to say that our Miss Ociee needs to become a young lady. It's the getting to that point that's making for the problem. She's fighting me something fierce about it."

Then, wiping his eyes, he managed a laugh. "Of course, maybe she thinks turning into a lady is nearly about as painful as cutting off this nice nose of hers." Papa tickled my nose.

"Ociee, dear, you'll like wearing pretty dresses and ribbons and you won't want to run after trains."

"Papa, is that why? Is it because Ben and I jumped for a ride on that boxcar? We haven't done it a single time since, I swear, cross my heart, that's forever true," I pleaded. "I'll just stay put in our house every day, I promise, Papa, every day."

"Oh, Miss Ociee, I'm not punishing you. It's simply that between trains and gypsies and no women around to care for you properly and your clumsy old father trying to hold us all together, I get so bewildered. This decision is about to tear my heart right out of my chest."

"Oh, Papa, me too."

"Would somebody please let me in on the riddle? What's going on?" demanded Ben.

Fred spoke up. "Ociee is going visit Aunt Mamie in Asheville for a while. She'll learn to do lady's things like sewing or fixing fancy food. And Ociee is going to school in Asheville, too, didn't Aunt Mamie say so, Papa, with other girls?"

I was feeling better hearing Fred talk with Ben, but Ben was acting confused. "Asheville! Asheville? And why would Ociee even *want* to be with silly girls, when she has me?" he questioned, his voice tapering off, "Asheville?".

Papa responded, "Ben, once you get more accustomed to the idea, you'll feel better about it. You've just now heard about this. Time has a way of making things right. For today, this is something you will understand better once you get older."

"I'm going to have to be a mighty old man to understand everything that's happening to me these days," replied Ben.

Papa said, "I know, son."

As scared as I was of leaving, I was even more worried for Ben. It would take him a mighty long while to come to grips with another person going away from his family. We were silent.

"Saying this got a lump out of my chest," sighed Papa, "I'd like to tell you children a story on myself. I practiced how to explain this way out in the middle of the corn field a day or two ago. It went a good deal better with those stalks than it did with you. I suppose corn doesn't tend to talk back as much as do you three."

"Oh, Papa," I giggled.

"Now let's get us all back up in the wagon and be about the fun we have ahead today," he proclaimed.

Papa, Ben, and I crowded on the seat together. Fred got in the back.

"Giddy up, Maude," we ordered.

Handing Ben the reins, Papa reached in his pocket for his harmonica. Papa had only been playing it for a few months. When he first showed it to us, he said he needed a lot of practice, and he was right. Hearing Papa play that harmonica was one of the very first times we all laughed together after we lost Mama.

Papa started to play. And we had to laugh again. Together we sang, "She'll be comin' round the mountain when she comes, she'll be coming round the mountain when she comes . . .

Fred added a new verse, "She'll be wearing frilly dresses when she comes, she'll be wearing frilly dresses when she comes *home.*"

Papa sang out *"home"* real loud and waved his harmonica high above his head. Reflections from it caught the sun and made my eyes squint.

"Yes, Papa, when I come home," I said. "When I come home."

"You are so right, Miss Ociee, what a fine day that will be! That is if you even will want to come back to this dusty old farm after spending time in a good place like Asheville."

"Papa, I know I will."

Ben chimed in, "Papa, could I go along with Ociee to protect her on the train?"

Papa said, "Ben, Ociee will be plenty safe, and we need for you to be here with Fred and with me. Besides, son, your school will open soon."

Ben really started to sulk when that sank in.

"Ben, don't be a ninny, I'll do all right. I'll ride that train like Aunt Mamie did. She didn't have you with her either."

Ben snapped the reins on Maude's harness. "I just wanted to go along, that's what."

Papa put his arm around both Ben and me. "Ben, the fact is Fred and I couldn't bear to let the both of you go at the same time."

We weren't in the habit of arguing with Papa about serious matters. We didn't say more. Until, almost afraid to hear his answer, I asked anyway, "When, Papa, when do I have to leave?"

6

Once again, Papa took a deep breath. "Ociee, I kept putting off telling you for so many days that I'm sorry to tell you it's coming soon, in just two weeks."

Two weeks, two weeks, two weeks. His words echoed across the dusty road to Abbeville.

"My dear Ociee, I have money with me today for the purchase of your ticket." The August sun beamed down on our wagon as Maude trotted toward town. Not one of us, not even Ben, could say a word.

We pulled up to the Abbeville railroad station. Usually it was a treat going there on a regular day. This time was different.

"Morning, Mr. Nash," said the man behind the tall wooden desk. "This must be your little girl."

"Yes, indeed," beamed Papa.

"Ociee, I'm Mr. Hall. Your Papa has come to this station two times already to plan thoroughly all the details regarding your trip to Asheville.

"Yes, sir," I said.

Papa put his arm around me as Mr. Hall talked about the train. He said, "It takes a big girl, one like you, to embark on such a grand adventure. The trip will take a whole day and night. Rest assured, you'll keep occupied watching out the window to see the interesting sights go by."

I listened politely.

Mr. Hall said the car I'd ride in had leather seats. The scary part was when he told me about how I would have to change onto another train in Chattanooga. Chattanooga is a big town, he told me.

"My daughter, Ociee Nash, will manage very well," Papa assured me, Mr. Hall and, as always, himself. "It is simply a matter of gaining confidence," Papa would repeat many times in the days to come.

Ben was beginning to sulk. He was jealous, something awful. After all, Fred had once ridden on a train all the way to Memphis. Papa and Mama had traveled by train many times. Of course, they had made the same trip I would be making, except only backwards. Or was I the one who was going backwards? Whichever way, I surely wished Ben would be with me on the train and so did he.

Mr. Hall told us about the conductor who walks up and down the train aisle seeing to the comforts of all his passengers. He said, "It's his job to help you, so you be sure to ask him about anything you need or want. Fact is, I used to be a conductor myself, and children were always my favorites."

"Ociee, what do you think?" asked Papa.

I told him, "It's all right. Thank you, Mr. Hall."

Papa knew "it's all right" was what I said when I was still thinking things over.

"Mr. Nash, I want you to know that Ociee will be well looked after on her trip." Mr. Hall insisted.

Papa nodded and told him I'd be fine. I tried to look bigger. Papa took money out of his leather pouch and gave it to Mr. Hall. In return, Mr. Hall handed him my ticket for "safe-keeping."

Mr. Hall waved good-bye, "We'll see you bright and early, 8 o'clock, the first day of September, Miss Nash. "

"Now, let's go send a telegram to Aunt Mamie to tell her you are really coming, Ociee," suggested Papa.

Fred said he believed he already knew what he needed to know about telegrams. He puffed up like our old rooster and crowed, "Think I'll just get me down the street and call on Rebecca."

Ben and I followed Papa into the telegraph office.

Papa stepped toward the desk. Motioning us over, he said, "Now, see what I'm doing? Be sure to hold your message to under ten words so the telegram won't cost more than 50 cents. Even at that, 50 cents is mighty high, if you ask me."

We watched Papa's every movement as he wrote down his message:

Miss Mamie Nash, 66 Charlotte Street, Asheville, North Carolina STOP
Ociee to arrive 1 PM September 2 STOP
Love George STOP

"See, nine words," he said.

"Papa, did you write *stop* every time because you've changed your mind about me going to Aunt Mamie's?"

Papa laughed, "Oh no, Ociee, that's the way to send a telegraph. You have to put the word *stop* in between each sentence to send the message clearly through those wires that connect to the telegraph stations."

"I guess I must have decided I do want to go after all, because when I saw the stop part, I felt sad."

"That's my girl."

We gave the message to the telegraph operator and watched as he tapped out the message out on his machine. "Diittt-dotttt-diiitttt."

Ben decided he just might grow up and do that job. He said it would be a lot more interesting than milking cows.

"Good idea, Ben. Now, why don't you and Ociee walk around while I get some nails and a few items on my list? We can meet back at the store in 30 minutes. Here, who will carry my pocket watch? The future seamstress or the future telegraph operator?"

"I will, Papa, since I'll be riding the train in two weeks."

"Very well, I will see you two at 10:30 at Mr. Jones' store."

I felt proud that he trusted me with his watch.

Papa started down the wood sidewalk when he turned around. "Ociee, Ben, I heard that Mr. Jones has in some maple sugar pralines from New Orleans, see if he might be willing to sell us some."

Ben shouted, "Race you there."

Ben wasn't a telegraph operator just yet and I wasn't a seamstress. We ran fast, even faster than when that old gypsy was after us.

7

Word that we had bought my ticket spread like wildfire throughout the community. Papa said Aunt Mamie probably heard our news without need of a telegram. People who hardly knew me were talking to us about my trip and giving every possible piece of travel advice they could dream up. What to take, how to sleep, when to eat—I wondered if I were the first girl ever to travel east from Mississippi. Papa said I was the *most extraordinary* one to do so.

We decided that, although folks were well intentioned, we should settle down to our normal routine for a few days. The boys had to begin the fall planting, and I wanted to start my packing and planning for the train ride itself. I longed for peaceful time to say good-bye to home. Most importantly, however, I had to continue to search the house, the garden, the barn, the fields and woods, every place I could think of, for Mama's lost locket. It'd certainly be too late once I was living in Asheville. I trembled at the thought. Deep in my heart, I believed that her locket would give me courage.

Ben also made good on his promise to keep searching. He even traced our run backwards to the place where I fell down running from the gypsy. He said he traced our path all the way back down to Miller's Creek and into the camp. There was something in me that didn't quite believe the "into the camp" part.

The reality was that Mama's locket was good and gone. But I wasn't ready to face that. Not just yet.

Midafternoon on a nice quiet day, I stayed in the house to begin trying to put my things in the steamer trunk. It was a funny feeling to pack my winter coat and it still August. It was hot in Mississippi, but Papa said the mountains got cold sooner.

Ben was green when he heard I would get to see snow during the winter.

Let's see, I'm for sure taking my quilt that Mama made, so that was not to be packed. Oh no. That'll go with me on the train.

"Woo hoo, anybody home? It's me, Miss May."

"I'm right here, Miss May," I said. Not quiet now, I thought as I ran through the parlor to the front door. When she hugged me, it was like being inside a chicken dumpling. Miss May even smelled like her kitchen. Her white cotton apron was dotted with sugar sprinkles and fresh churned butter. She almost always had flour in her hair.

"Oh, Ociee, honey, Miss May is going to miss you, you sweet, pretty little motherless thing."

Fred always said Miss May had the funniest way of turning a kind act into a sad occasion. But Papa said she certainly meant well and had a good heart.

"I brought you a pound cake for today, precious child. Now this is for every one of you Nashes, but honey, when you get ready for your train trip, I'm going to have a whole tin of my special butter shortbread cookies just for you. Oh dear, I do hope you'll be safe traveling all that long, long way."

Once again, she nearly took my last wind with her hug. My face was buried in her big bosom. Miss May left in a flurry of jiggling fat and many more "oh dears" as she worried out loud about train wrecks. It was amazing to me how someone so fat could move so fast.

I went back to sorting my things. I'd pack my dungarees. I was sure Aunt Mamie would want her flowers looked after, especially if she had roses. Dungarees would be perfect for yard work.

Suddenly, I heard a noise. The front door creaked and swung open. Someone was in our house.

"Miss May, is it you? Did you forget something?"

No answer.

My heart pounded. I whispered, "Miss May?" Again, nothing.

What if it was a hobo coming for food? Papa and Fred warned me about hoboes. I was all alone. Crouched down beside my bed, I heard the sound of heavy feet walking through the parlor. It was a man.

I tried to say, "Papa or Fred." My mouth was open but nothing came out. I hid way back underneath my bed.

I tried to pray. "Lord make us thankful." The heavy boots clomped into the kitchen. It was a hobo all right, and he must have been looking for food. There was breakfast toast and sausage on the table. I thought, "Please take the food. "

Miss May's pound cake, oh no! It was in there with me. He'd smell it and come for it — and me. I was still as a little mouse, I heard my own heart — thump, bump. I might as well just say, "Here I am, Mr. Hobo, come get me." I wished I was already in Asheville with Aunt Mamie, and with no hoboes anywhere in sight.

Then the boots came toward my bed. They stopped. I could barely see from under my coverlet. Take the cake, just take it! Miss May could make another cake, there's just one Ociee.

It was not a hobo.

Those boots, those boots belonged to the gypsy! He was in my room. I held my breath as he moved closer. "Can't hold it, can't, can't," I let it go with a loud "pffftt." He spun around and stomped those heavy feet toward my hiding place. He lifted the cover and looked me right in the eye.

"What is thees, a frightened rabbeet, I theenk."

With that I scurried out, jumped right on top of my bed and shouted, "I am not a rabbit, I am Ociee Nash, and you are in my house." My heart was about to shoot out right through my neck.

"Ah, yes, like you were in my camp with zee leettle freend, Miss Ladiee?"

"Well, I suppose so. Ben, Ben's my brother — Ben and I were there. And he and Papa, my great big Papa, and Fred, my even bigger big brother will be here any minute. You can't kidnap me. There," I pointed to Miss May's basket, "take the cake and go."

With that the gypsy started to laugh. It wasn't the deep scary laugh I remembered. It was more of a Papa kind of laugh. Then he said, "Not before I geeve you thees."

He reached into his pocket and unfolding his big brown hand, he revealed Mama's locket.

"I theenk you leeve thees when you and the boy run away from me."

Still standing straight up in the middle of my bed, I reached out toward the locket. Our eyes met. Those weren't the eyes of a fire breathing monster.

The gypsy and I stood and concentrated on one another for what seemed like a very long time.

My mind flashed back to a bear we saw in the circus in Holly Springs last year. Long before the circus came, posters advertised all the acts. We read about high wire artists, about clowns and elephants, but mostly Ben and I wanted to see that bear:

Giant Kodiak Bear
10-foot tall, ferocious monster
12,000 pounds of fear!

We couldn't wait. We talked about him for weeks. When Papa took us to Holly Springs, the first thing we did was to race to his cage. Well, that bear just grunted and yawned and waddled to his food dish. Not a tooth in his mouth.

We were crushed. Ben said the "ferocious beast" likely had to gum his food. "Our milk cows are scarier than that bear," he had joked.

Oh, the gypsy had teeth all right. I could tell when he smiled, but he didn't scare me anymore. He just looked big and brown and very gentle, gentle like that bear.

The gypsy leaned toward me and laid Mama's locket on my fingertips. Then he wrapped all ten of his rough fingers around my hand and said, "There you are, Miss Ladiee. You must take care not to lose thees. You may not again be so fortunate as to get back thee heart on eets leettle chain."

He turned and walked toward the door.

I clutched the locket in both hands. I brushed it with my lips, "It's back, oh Mama, our locket is back."

"Oh dear me." I started after the gypsy and shouted, "Sir, wait a minute, sir!" I am sorry. I forgot to thank you."

"So, Miss Ladiee, yes, you are welcome, I weel say."

"No, that's not enough. Here come into our parlor. Wait, please wait, just a minute." I ran back into my room. I picked up Miss May's basket with the pound cake. "Here you go. Now I can thank you properly for the trouble you took. This is from me and from Mama."

He took the basket and, smelling its contents, said, "Hmm, your MaaMaa ees a good baker woman, I theenk."

"Oh, no, Mama didn't bake this. Miss May did. She always bakes things for us and puts them in this same basket. Oh, please, can you remember to bring her basket back to us?"

"Oh, but to be sure, Miss Ladiee, thees I weell."

"Mama died."

The gypsy stood silently. It seemed the right thing to tell him. He listened.

"That's Mama's picture over the desk, except Mama should be smiling. She always did, but they don't paint smiles on formal pictures, Papa says. The measles killed my Mama last spring. Folks said, 'the measles epidemic hit our county real bad,' but we think it hit us the worst. I don't believe things will ever seem right to us Nashes again, but Papa says they will. He says us Nashes are strong people."

A red bandanna held back the gypsy's dark curly hair. His gold earring touched his shoulder when he bowed his head. He watched me through brown eyes which seemed as deep as our well.

"How sorry I am for you, Miss and for your famelee," he whispered.

I kept talking, "That's what made it so awful about losing the locket. It was Mama's. Papa and my Aunt Mamie gave it to me after Mama's funeral."

"Theese, I understand," he nodded. "I am all the happieest that eet ees found for you."

"Where, sir, did you find it?" I asked.

He said, "I theenk, in your great hurry to leeve my home, you failed to see eet drop from around your leetle neck. I see eet as I clean around my spot yesterdee. I couldn't dream from where eet come to me. Then I remember your short veset. I breeng to you."

He looked again at Mama's portrait, and we walked out on the front porch. He gazed at me and said, "I see much sadness for the heart of one yeet so small."

I wiped my cheek. "Oh, I'm not so small. I'm going on a train all by myself to Asheville, North Carolina. In fact, my train leaves from Abbeville on September 1st, early in the morning. Ben, you know Ben. Ben wanted to go too, but Papa said no to that."

The gypsy reared back his head and laughed, "I see you are not the frightened rabbeet at all, not like the day at my camp! I wish you well, Miss Ladiee, een your travels to that place, Asheveele."

He left as quickly as he had come.

I wanted to ask him about his travels, about the painting on his wagon. Did his earring hurt? I should have asked, for Ben's sake, if he stole children. But I knew that my gypsy would never do such a thing, not my gypsy.

I was talked out. It was as if I were out of air. All I could do was stand silently by and watch as he started down the dirt path. His horse was hitched to our fence way down near the smoke house. No wonder I hadn't heard anything. Untying the big black animal, the gypsy mounted and firmly hooked Miss May's basket on the saddle horn. He slapped his horse's rump and trotted away. Turning, the man waved farewell. I could see his smile, it sparkled even that far from my eyes.

I went inside. That afternoon had been like a dream. I wandered back to my room and stood in front of the mirror over my washstand. Reaching in my apron pocket, I removed the hankie. I held my breath. What if this hadn't happened at all. I had wished it to be real. No gypsy ever really came. The locket wasn't in my pocket after all. I reached inside my apron.

I touched the tiny heart. It *was* still there. Pulling it out, I gripped it ever so tight. Hooking it around my neck, I vowed, "I will never, ever let you out of my sight again."

I felt put back together now that I had Mama's locket around my neck.

"Now, Ociee Nash, you'd best get busy." Where did I put my Sunday stockings?

8

"Ociee, Ociee," shouted Fred. "I'm home. Let's get supper going. Ociee? Papa's on his way, too. Ociee? Where are you, girl?"

I just prissed in the kitchen with a grin on my face. I had the locket tucked under my collar.

"Hello, Fred, where is that Ben?"

"Why, he's with Papa. What's your hurry?"

"Oh, just wondering." I wasn't accustomed to lying to anybody, especially to my big brother, but my news would have to wait for the whole family. Fred was getting suspicious. I was becoming nervous. Thankfully, we saw Papa and Ben coming up in the wagon.

As Papa walked up toward the house, we noticed he was carrying a parcel. Ben bolted up the back steps two at a time.

"Ociee, we got something for the new lady!"

Papa and Ben were grinning so much we knew they were up to something. Papa handed me the package which was all wrapped up fancy in white paper with a pink bow ribbon on top.

I held it close and looked at Ben. I figured he would blurt out what it was, but, for once, he didn't tell. They all wanted me to rip off the paper, but I wouldn't do any such thing because I wanted to stretch out every second of my surprise. Nobody ever got a present unless it was Christmas or a birthday.

It was easy to see that Papa was as pleased he could be. He told me that he and Ben bought my gift at Fitch's Mercantile in Abbeville. Mrs. Fitch herself helped them pick it out, and she wrapped it up special for "Ociee Nash to use on her journey to Asheville."

I couldn't wait another second. Being real careful, I removed the bow and put it aside to save. Next I tore off the white paper and opened the lid of the stiff paper hat box. I reached inside.

"Oh, Papa, it's a hat, a real lady's hat!"

I took it out. It was straw with a light blue sash that would tie into a bow under my chin. Just over the brim there were little paper roses with green leaves.

Ben was about to pop. He said, "Do you like it, Ociee?"

"Oh yes, Ben. Thank you all! I will wear it on the train and in Asheville and be a lady like Aunt Mamie. She says ladies always wear hats, right, Papa? "

Papa grinned his yes and said, "Ociee, there's good things to becoming more girlish, don't you see?"

"I guess that might be so after all, Papa."

Papa took the hat from my hands and pointed out the pink flowers on the front of the brim. "I had Mrs. Fitch add these special for my Miss Ociee," he said. He put the hat on my head and said, "Now let us men folk have a look."

I put it on and tied the sash under my chin.

Papa spoke first, "Ociee, you are just about the most beautiful sight I ever saw. Your Mama would be as proud as I am. Fact is, my shirt buttons are close to popping off because my chest is puffed like that prideful old rooster out back."

Ben was next to comment. "Oh no! You already *do* look like a girl, Ociee! Take it off!"

Then Fred added his say. "Well, you're nearly as pretty as Rebecca."

"I hope I'm as pretty as Rebecca, *my calf*." I laughed and everyone laughed with me.

"Yes sir," said Papa. "Things are starting to look up for this family of ours. I have two strong boys and a fine, almost ten-year old daughter. I am indeed a happy man this evening."

Ben said, "Ociee, I'm glad you like your hat, but Papa, can we get to our supper now? I'm starving because I can hear my stomach grumbling. It says 'Feed Ben now.'"

"Of course we can, Ben."

I asked to be excused for just a minute. I wanted to see my new hat on me, too, and without everybody looking on. I strutted out of the kitchen and into my room to take my own look in the wash stand mirror.

Yes, it was a truly beautiful hat. And Ben was right. I looked more ladylike already and older, too, at least every bit of ten or eleven, *maybe*. I remembered Mama's locket.

I raced back into the kitchen where they all were busy with getting supper together.

"All right, I'm back. Here, I'll set the table. Oh, Papa, Ben, Fred. Guess what else happened today?"

Papa turned around from the sink. Ben looked up from peeling potatoes. Fred stopped carving chicken.

I slowly took off my new hat and placed it with the pink ribbon in the Fitch's box. I closed the lid and carefully placed it on an empty shelf. I was enjoying the suspense. They watched every move I made.

Papa, looking worried, asked, "What is it, Ociee?"

I produced the locket. "Look what the gypsy found and brought to me."

Papa grabbed my shoulders and said, "Thank the Lord!" He looked closely at Mama's tiny gold heart and touched it with his trembling finger. He uttered, "Ociee, did I hear you right? Did you say the gypsy was here, here in our home? That same gypsy who chased you and Ben down at Miller's Creek?"

For the first time, Ben was totally speechless.

I told them that the gypsy wasn't scary one little bit. Ben looked at me with his mouth hanging open. Still no words.

"He came into our house?" repeated Papa. "Ociee, he didn't frighten you, did he?"

"At first he did, Papa," I admitted, "but then I realized he just came by to return Mama's locket. "

After I told them the whole story, Ben blurted out, "He didn't as much as try to steal you away?"

"Ben," I said, "you sound disappointed!"

Papa said he believed there must be a lot of good in a man to go to all that trouble for our family. He looked at Ben and then at me and then he cupped Mama's locket in his hand.

"I think we should all rejoice that this treasure has finally found its way home. Children, I hope you've learned something about people. Never decide if a person is bad or good based on how he looks on the outside. Ben, hear me?"

We said we understood, but Ben was pouting. He puffed up, "I can't get over Ociee seeing that old gypsy without me even being here."

"Ben," I said, "you might be at home when the gypsy brings the basket back."

"When he brings the basket back? Is he coming here again? When?! I'll be ready! Wait, what basket?" Ben asked.

"Why Miss May's basket that she brought us with a cake inside," I said. "But I don't know exactly when he'll be back."

Ben cried out, "You gave away a cake Miss May baked?"

Fred said, "Ben, you've forgotten what Papa just said."

"Guess I don't understand how looking for good in people had much to do with *somebody* giving away *my* cake."

We sat down to eat supper. As we ate, Papa told us he decided we would only do the most necessary chores the morning of my trip. Once he said those words, the fact of my actual leaving began to set in with us.

Fred asked how my packing was coming along and my eyes filled with tears.

Papa put down his fork and said, "Ben, run down to the gypsy's camp and tell him Ben Nash wants his cake back. Don't you take 'no' for an answer."

Ben's eyes were big as the supper plates. "You mean it, Papa, do you really want me to go?"

Papa laughed first, then Fred. I believed Papa was serious at first. Then when even Ben snickered, I had to giggle, too.

That was to be the last evening meal we four had together. After that night, neighbors were always asking me to eat with them or bringing supper to join us or having Papa and me over.

Papa explained it was to send me off with the well wishes of our community. I would have been happier if we had just been *us*, just me and Papa, Ben and Fred.

9

Before I knew it, I woke up to "Cock-a-doodle-Ociee" for my last morning in my own bed. I said "woke up," but the fact was I had twisted around in my bed covers all night long. I couldn't remember doing any sleeping to wake up from on September 1, 1898. Part of me was excited. Part of me was afraid. All of me wanted to go, but all of me wanted to stay right there on the farm with my Papa and two brothers.

Getting out of bed, I pulled up the sheets. I carefully folded Mama's quilt and put it on top of my packed trunk. One of the farm ladies had made me a new puffy sleeved cotton dress for my trip. Monday, when she brought it by, Fred suggested that she was trying to show Aunt Mamie that Mississippi women could sew as good as North Carolina women. Papa said that may be, but he thought she sewed it to have me look my very best to travel so Mama would have been proud. I didn't understand either of them. I just liked the flowers on the dress. They matched the ones on my hat from Fitch's Mercantile.

I slipped the dress over my head, brushed my hair and put on Mama's locket. A tag on my dress told who I was and where I was going. Papa had written it out last night. It read:

"Miss Ociee Nash, age 9 years, daughter of George Nash from Abbeville, Mississippi, going to Miss Mamie Nash, 66 Charlotte Street, Asheville, North Carolina.

Papa told me I would have to wear it for the entire trip. I looked in the mirror. "You can do it, Ociee Nash, you can do this all by yourself."

After breakfast we left dishes soaking in the pan of heated water. Fred carried my trunk out to the wagon. Papa had already hitched up Maude to the wagon. He called us to get a move on.

I hurried through our house one more time so I could remember how it all looked. I needed to see it in my memory if I were to get lonesome at Aunt Mamie's. Then I said good-bye to home, placed my new hat on my head, went outside and climbed aboard the wagon.

Ben was fussing more than usual. "Here I am wearing my Sunday clothes, and it isn't even Sunday," he sulked.

"Ben, you're just fuming because I'm going on the train without you."

"That's not true," he fired back. "Fact is, school starts next week. That's all. I don't care about any old train and not about missing you either."

We drove down the dirt road to Abbeville. It looked like it might rain later in the day. Papa didn't even think to play his harmonica.

We rode real quiet for a long spell. I kept looking hard at everything as we passed by the neighbors' farms, houses, and fields. I wanted to remember every tree, every barn, every cow.

"What will become of my calf?" I shouted.

At first my hollering made everyone jump.

Fred reminded me he volunteered. He said, "Remember, I promised that while you're away, Ociee, I will look after *both* Rebeccas."

"Oh, Fred, that makes me feel some better," I sighed.

Ben said, "I hope Rebecca in Abbeville won't be getting as fat as Ociee's calf! But I bet you she will if she keeps eating all that candy Fred takes to her every Sunday." Ben was back to being Ben. I was glad.

"Hush up, Ben," Fred said. He was blushing about that.

For just a little time, we were all us again. Even so, the remainder of our trip into town was very, very silent.

Before I could even believe it, Papa, said, "Whoa, slow down, Maude. We're about there, Miss Ociee." When we pulled up at the train station, Papa had Ben help Fred with my trunk.

Papa turned in the driver's seat. He placed his hands on my hat and straightened it. I don't think it was even crooked. There hadn't been much of a wind that morning.

Crossing his arms across his chest, he said, "My, but you are so pretty this fine September day. You do our family proud."

"Oh, Papa." I hugged him tight.

"Dear daughter of mine, you'll arrive there with Aunt Mamie before you think you have as much as left Mississippi. Mind you now, make certain Mamie telegraphs us to say you're there. Have her send the wire as soon as she can 'cause we will be most anxious."

"Yes, Papa."

"You have your hair brush, sandwiches, cookies, and spending money in your coin purse. Is your tag still pinned on good and straight?"

"Yes, Papa."

Fred and Ben bounded around the corner. They were chattering some silliness, but I didn't care. I already felt far away from them.

"Remember, the conductor will answer any questions you can possibly think of asking. Don't be too shy now, Ociee. Mr. Hall told me that his name is Mr. Charles."

"Yes, Papa."

"Ociee, look at me. Hold your chin up," he said.

"If I hold my chin up my neck will get all loose and I'll cry," I told him. With that my tears started to flow. Papa grabbed me close. Fred ran over. Ben followed. The four of us stood in the middle of the Abbeville train station, arms wrapped around each other and we cried.

Our anguish came to a cold screeching halt when a man's voice bellowed, "All Aboard."

Papa and the boys walked me all the way up the steps and into the train, right to my seat. Papa told me to sit next to the window. Then he put my basket of food and the quilt next to me so I had my own "little bird's nest" as he called it. He leaned over and pointed out exactly where to look so I'd see all of them waving at me.

"Yes, Papa."

He told the boys to bid me good-bye.

Fred picked me up and squeezed me close. "Oh my back! I won't be able to lift you come spring." He put me down and winked.

Ben started to hug me, but he didn't.

"Bye," he said.

"Bye," I said.

I had never felt so hollow. At least not until Papa said he'd best kiss me one more time. Then even Papa turned and left. He looked back and smiled but he didn't smile big.

I searched the station platform as Papa said to do. There came Fred with Ben by his side. Papa was hurrying to his place with my brothers. He was doing his best to be excited about my trip. I hoped he'd walk right up those steps and grab me off the train. I saw him put his arm around Ben.

Poor Ben. He wasn't jealous of my train ride at all. He was too sad to be anything else but sad.

I waved, but I was neither thrilled nor brave. I couldn't be. Ben was sobbing. One more person was leaving him. This time it was me.

The train pulled out of Abbeville.

10

I watched Papa and the boys as they got smaller and smaller. Don't shrink away, oh, don't be gone from me. But it was no use. Before another minute, even the station shrank until it was swallowed up by the black smoke from the train's engine.

I stared out my window. At first I thought my leftover tears were blurring the passing trees and fields. I couldn't as much as make out a single corn stalk. Fields looked like patches of green. Here I was, raised on a farm, and I couldn't tell beans from corn except that the corn was taller.

The boxcar that Ben and I had jumped on was going mighty slow compared to the ride I was having in the passenger car. Fred told me trains speed up as they move out from town, but this train must have been traveling two times as fast as it should have. I got dizzy. My stomach was twirling. I reached to hold Mama's locket and it steadied me a bit.

I kept watching out. I would try to look at one big tree, but quick as I saw it, it would zip backwards away from me. That reminded me of fanning fast through a picture book. There was a barn, then it was gone. A cow was watching me go by. "Look out, old cows. We'll surely mow you down," I cried out. There was a silo and then a house. The house looked a tiny bit like ours. Whoosh, it disappeared.

I reached for Mama's quilt. I looked out the window. Mama had put together little pieces of dresses and shirts to make her quilt. So much like hers, the passing barns and fields and fences and animals were stitched together to make a giant's quilt-like pattern of my state of Mississippi. I clutched the quilt.

"Good morning, Miss Nash," said the conductor. My day-dreaming interrupted, I sat ramrod straight in my seat just like when the teacher surprised me in school.

He smiled at me and said, "Didn't mean to startle you, Miss Nash, I wanted to see if you'd be needing anything?"

"Oh, no thank you, sir," I said. "I just never have seen trees move so quick."

He laughed. "You can credit our big engine with that. Now you know to call on me for anything at all. My name is Mr. Charles."

"Yes sir, I will, Mr. Charles."

I was beginning to feel just a tiny bit better. The train had only a few passengers that morning. I noticed a man with a leather case. I asked about him.

Mr. Charles said, "Why, miss, he is a traveling salesman. He and fellows like him go all about the countryside on trains like ours peddling their wares. Ask him, I'm certain he would be happy to sell you a thing or two out of his bag there."

"Oh, I don't think so. I'd best not spend anything, just yet," I said as I fingered my purse with Papa's trip money.

Mr. Charles told me the salesman said he would be getting off to call on the big dry goods store in Holly Springs. He explained we'd have to stop many times along the way to take on coal and water and other supplies. I acted like I knew all about that. "Yes, Papa told me."

The train's first stop with me on board was to be Holly Springs.

"We went to Holly Springs to see the circus. Have you ever been to the circus, Mr. Charles? " I asked.

"Not since I was a boy, I'm sorry to say." He walked up the aisle. I watched him and wondered if he was ever really a boy. I had never seen a boy with a beard like that and he was pretty fat, too, as I thought about it. Of course, there were fat children at school, just no boys with beards.

I looked around and noticed an older lady sitting closer to the front of our passenger car. She was reading. I thought about Aunt Mamie and hoped that lady wasn't traveling to a funeral. I decided she must be on this train to go somewhere for a happy reason just like I was. At least, I hoped my journey to Asheville was for a good reason.

I decided to work harder on not thinking of home. Oh, I hoped Rebecca would remember me. My thoughts raced by to the rhythm of the choo-chooing of the train.

We began to slow down. I was glad Mr. Charles had explained that we were supposed to stop, otherwise, I would have gotten concerned. We were hardly moving as we came into the station.

Mr. Charles told me I could step off for fifteen minutes to stretch my legs but not to go far. We would know to come back and get settled into our seats when he called 'All aboard.'

"Mind you, Miss Nash, you listen out for my voice."

"Yes sir, I sure will."

I walked down the steps and out onto the platform. It was like Abbeville, but bigger and many more people were walking around. I would stick close to the train. It was then I heard a familiar voice.

"Miss Ladiee, Miss Ladiee, over theese way," he said.

Never had I imagined I'd see the gypsy in the train station in Holly Springs. It was him all right. Well beyond the train, in a grove of pine trees, I could see his wagon and his huge black horse.

The gypsy walked my way. The people around the station glared at him with fearful looks. I guess they didn't know about not judging folks by their outsides. Mr. Charles, looking like our sheriff in Marshall County, ran over as if to head off the gypsy's attack.

"It's fine, Mr. Charles, he's my friend."

"If you say so, Miss Nash, but I'll stand right over here, just the same."

The gypsy never as much as slowed his steps. Soon we stood together face to face smack dab in the middle of the Holly Springs railroad station.

"What in the world are you doing here?" I asked.

"Thee time for me to move along ees also here for me, Miss Ladiee. I remember thees was to be your day of journey. You said I must return thees to you." He handed me Miss May's cake basket.

I took it and looked into the gypsy's eyes.

"The cake was very good to my taste," he said putting his big brown hands on his belly. "I eat all of eet, as you can see." He tilted back his head and shook his long black curls. Then he gave a loud laugh. His earring caught the sunlight.

I looked at the growing crowd of at least twenty people including Mr. Charles. I ignored their stares.

"See, I'm wearing Mama's locket."

The gypsy smiled.

"I return the basket to you. Now look weethen for I have for you a geft of my choice. I do so to please my little freend," he explained.

I turned back a red piece of fabric and looked at what was inside. Down in the bottom I found a small picture which was painted on a piece of carved pine. It was a painting of a lady. Gently taking it out, I examined it closely. It was Mama. Best of all, it was Mama with a smile. Healthy. I could remember her then, clear as a bell.

"It's the most beautiful thing I ever saw! Mama, Mama's face. How could you know?" I asked.

He replied, "I theenk of her as she appear in her portrait. Theen I paint the sparkles I see in her girl child's face. That, Miss Ladiee, shows us both your Mama as shee be," said he.

"Oh," I swooned finding my own eyes in Mama's for the first time. Thrilled, I then noticed something else, "And, her dress, it's lavender. Mama's favorite color was lavender, but how could you know that?"

"Oh, Miss Ladiee, the weemen, they like the garden colors as do you, I theenk. I know how much you wanted to see your Mama joy-filled so I do eet for you. Now I must leeve from thees place. Farewell to you, my freend and a safe journey." He turned away.

54

I ran beside him and grabbed his elbow. "Wait, I don't as much as know your name."

"My name to you matters not, that I am your freend ees the theeng of emportance. For that I weell say, as before, you are most welcome."

He walked toward his horse and wagon. Turning around, he said, "Perhaps one day we weell cross paths agean."

As on the day at our farm, I watched as my gypsy friend left. This time he didn't mount the huge black horse. This time the horse pulled his wagon. I caught one last glimpse of the beautiful painted lady on the wagon's side.

"Geet up, geet up, you fine black beast," he snapped the reins, the horse responded immediately as it pulled the gypsy, house and all, away from the pine grove and out on to the road headed north.

Mr. Charles came to me and said, "Miss Nash, looking after you might be more of a responsibility than I had originally thought."

I smiled up at him. "I'm certain that I will meet no more gypsies, sir. And, Mr. Charles, as you can see, I am fine and dandy."

"Yes, ma'am, that I can see."

I returned to my seat. I didn't want to have Mr. Charles call for me, so I was the first person settled in my place. Looking around, I noticed the first salesman had gotten off, but he had been replaced by another who looked pretty much like him. The lady was back in her same seat. She must have observed my conversation with the gypsy, because she looked at me like I had a tail. I made up my mind not to tell anyone about my friend. It was more fun causing folks to wonder.

"All aboard that's coming aboard!"

A boy and his mother got on the train. He stopped and poked his finger at my face. "See, that's her, Ma. That's the girl I saw with that old gypsy man."

"Now, you hush up, Sam. Don't you be pointing."

At first I giggled, then I missed Ben all over again.

To get my mind on something else, I opened the basket. I looked again at the painting. No bigger than the palm of Papa's hand, I would treasure that smiling Mama as long as I lived. One of these days I'd show it to Papa and the boys. And I soon would be able to show it to Aunt Mamie. How surprised she would be to hear about my friend the gypsy, my friend with no name.

I placed it back in the basket. The train pulled out of the station. The engineer blasted the train whistle. I realized I hadn't heard that whistle in Abbeville because of my crying. I settled back to look outside. Black smoke puffed up the engine's stack and thinned out past me. Holly Springs began to shrink, fade, and soon disappeared behind us. We went faster. Houses raced by, trees ran, cows blurred.

I spotted a rise on the flat Mississippi countryside. On the top, a square shape. A horse. A man. The man was waving a red bandanna. I shoved open the window as high as it would go. Hanging out far as I dared, I hollered, "Good-bye! Good-bye! Thank you, good bye!"

Over the chug of the train, I thought I heard, "Farewell, Miss Ladiiiieeee."

11

I had carried stories to read along the way, but like Mr. Hall had said, I found myself more drawn to what I was seeing outside. I couldn't shake the thought I would see Papa or Fred and Ben along one of the roads as we rumbled past. The farms looked pretty much like ours and those of our neighbors. It was the people who were not my people.

Children played on tree swings. But they weren't the children I ever played with.

Mamas shelled peas as they sat on back porches and watched the swinging. But these were different mamas. Dogs barked. I missed Gray Dog. Cows mooed. These only looked similar to Papa's.

The train chugged on the steel tracks. I was being pulled further away from Papa and the boys. I was now isolated from the things I knew and from the comfort of familiar faces.

I touched the wood framing the train's window. Tracing its grain, the patterns circled out like ripples. Around and around. Familiar somehow. My mind traveled back to another pattern of wood. Pine wood. The pine of Mama's coffin. I remembered trying to study those shapes rather than look at Mama's cold still face as she lay in that box, that pine box in the very front of our church. She couldn't have been Mama. She didn't look one bit like her. She looked like the porcelain doll in the window of Fitch's Mercantile.

Papa sat with us children on the first row. He could have stretched his legs long and touched the box. But instead, he had his feet, with his shoes freshly polished, tucked under the pew. First was me, then Papa, then Ben and Fred. Fred had to get up to carry Ben outside because he cried so hard he started choking. Papa held me so tight his arms were shaking. I just kept looking at those pine knots and whispering to myself, "You just jump out of there, Mama. Tell me this is a bad, awful dream. Get out of there and hold me, hold Papa and let's go get Fred and Ben."

The organ lady played hymns real slow that I could feel in the way deep part of my stomach. She had long bony fingers. It was hard to tell where her fingers left off and the keys of the organ began.

Why did my Mama have to die? Measles is a cruel sickness. Measles is a monster that hurts too many children and husbands and hurts whole families. I wish I had never heard that monster word. Measles. Horrors.

Aunt Mamie, will you seem like a *real* Mama for me? Will you act kind like you did when you came for Mama's funeral? Were you sure when you wrote to Papa that you wanted me there with you?

Papa and the boys must have gotten settled and working back home. Maybe they were sitting down to eat. Nobody had been hungry at breakfast. I could almost see Papa in his place at the table's head with Fred on his right and Ben in the middle. Wait. Middle of what? I wasn't there to be at the other end. Only my empty chair, no me. They probably have forgotten Ociee ever was theirs. I suddenly felt sad from the top of my new hat all the way down to the toes of my Sunday shoes.

I shifted around on the leather train seat. At first, the seat had felt slick-like. I could slide around pretty easy. Then, as I settled into it, it melted to me and I stuck. I yearned for grass to sit in or the rocker in the corner of our porch. I wanted to sit cross legged on my bed at home, yes, on my bed at home. That was where I should have been that day, that first day of September.

"Ociee!" I said to myself, "Of course, Papa and the boys are missing you something terrible. They must be grieving up a storm. What a silly girl you are." I unstuck myself from the seat.

Mr. Charles walked by checking tickets. He stopped at my seat.

"Near about out of Mississippi, Miss Nash. Mr. Hall back in Abbeville said you would want to know where we were along the way. So be on the lookout and soon I'll say that we have crossed over the state line into Tennessee." He gave me a wink and walked on ahead.

I had imagined the whole state would turn a different color when we left Mississippi. In Fred's geography book, Mississippi was orange and Tennessee was green. I knew Mississippi was *not* really orange all over, except in fall, and that was only the hickory and maple trees. Even though I was disappointed when it wasn't like Fred's book, green from end to end, just north of Mississippi.

"Welcome to Tennessee, ladies and gentlemen," Mr. Charles announced.

My heart began to pound. This was really happening. I was leaving Mississippi and Papa. And Tennessee was no greener than Mississippi was orange.

I looked down at the tag on my dress. The boys had made fun of me when Papa wrote it. Fred laughed at his own silly joke, "The train's delivery man will put you on Aunt Mamie's front porch and shout, 'Package for Miss Mamie Nash, Asheville. Delivery of goods from Marshall County, Mississippi, one Ociee Nash."

Papa had chuckled a little, but when he noticed that I didn't laugh, he said, "Now, Fred, our Ociee needs to board that train with a lofty opinion of her big brother. Best not to tease her today."

Most times it would have been all right for Papa to take up for me, but that day I wanted regular things to happen. I didn't want to be treated special. Everyone had to be extra nice because I was leaving. And I knew it.

I could feel the roar of the train in my feet. I'd put my toes down and roll back to my heels then the roar would ride to my knees. My whole body shook from the inside out. I felt I was becoming part of the car myself. The train and Ociee Nash chugged east across Tennessee.

I waved to the conductor, "Mr. Charles, could I trouble you with a question?"

"Yes, of course. That's why I'm here," he replied.

"Mr. Charles, is it possible that Tennessee is greener than Mississippi?" I asked.

He said, "I don't think so, unless, of course they had more rain up in these parts than did you folks in Mississippi. Don't reckon as I remember for sure."

I didn't really want to talk about the maps in Fred's book. I was only lonesome. I wanted to hear my own voice talk. And I was glad to hear Mr. Charles say something back, just to me.

I loved that train window, Ben would have, too. I wished for him to be there with me. We could have cheered as we watched the barns and the animals and the people and the trees speed pass our car. And we could have talked about all sorts of things, about home and about our trip and about how worried we were about going all the way to Asheville.

Mr. Charles suddenly leaned over my seat. "How are you doing?" he asked. I jumped to my feet.

He said, "Didn't mean to startle you again, Miss Nash, I have been so busy, I thought I might take a rest and ride here with you a spell. Would that suit you?"

I was mighty glad. I said, "Yes, sir, that will be fine, more than fine, it's extra special fine. Mr. Charles, I wish you wouldn't call me Miss Nash. I almost don't know who you're talking to when you call me that. Folks call me Ociee."

"Ah, that's pretty. Are you named after someone in your family?" he asked.

"No not family, I'm named after canned corn," I said.

"Whatever do you mean?" he laughed.

"It's a pet name. I'll tell you, *if* you want me to."

"Ociee, I reckon I got to hear this. You got my curiosity way up. These passengers may have to tend to themselves for a lengthy spell."

"My real name is Josephine, but when Ben, my brother was little, he couldn't say 'Josephine.' All Ben could get out was 'Josie' without the 'J.' That came out 'Ociee,' you see," I explained. Mama suggested we should spell it with an extra "e" because then I could be the only Ociee in the whole entire world. It gives me flair, don't you think?"

"Yes, I like that too. But what I don't quite see is where the corn figures in."

"Oh, that started the day Fred, my other brother, saw that *Oce Corn* on the store shelf. Somebody had gone and put my name on all his canned corn. "Of course, they didn't spell it just exactly correctly. Anyway, once Fred saw it, I was called 'Ociee Canned Corn' from that day and on. He would about laugh his head right off when he said it."

Mr. Charles was shaking his head, "I do declare."

"Of course, once Papa heard, you better believe, he called a stop to that! At least, whenever he was in earshot."

Mr. Charles laughed. He said he knew brothers were ugly to sisters without really meaning anything by it. He admitted he had acted terrible more than once towards his sisters.

I was surprised. "You, Mr. Charles, a nice train conductor like you. Imagine that?"

"I'm afraid so, Ociee," he replied.

"You're so kind now, Mr. Charles. Maybe Fred, and even Ben will be like you are when they're grown men."

"Oh, I 'spect they will, Ociee." He stood up and said, "Now, I'd best be seeing to the other passengers. Or they will not be thinking much of me as a conductor."

He tipped his conductor's hat at me like I was a grownup lady. Then Mr. Charles opened the door to a metal bridge that connected us to the next passenger car on down. Holding himself steady with the gates on either side of the bridge, he walked through to the next section and started checking on those people. I watched him as he went first to one person and then on to the next. Hmm, I wondered if girls could have important jobs like that. I'd be sure to look into doing some train work one day.

I liked Mr. Charles. He was gentlemanly and he was smart, just like Papa. I would remember to tell Papa when I wrote to him. "When I wrote to him!" It would seem so strange to *write* to Papa, because I was used to him being there at the kitchen table, or on the porch, or certainly no further away than our fields, or in Abbeville at the very worst.

I was suddenly hungry and decided to unwrap one of my strawberry sandwiches from home. I felt over the bread for Papa's finger indentions. Finding a couple of possible spots, I tried to touch where he had touched. I almost was tempted to save a bite so it wouldn't go completely away, but I ate it all anyway.

12

Our engine puffed a black haze that came and went like the mist that was over Papa's pond, but the train's smoke was hot and filthy dirty. Papa's pond was clean and cool to the smell.

"Here we come, toot, toot." The whistle sounded, "Tooo-woooo, there we go." The locomotive joggled our passenger cars as we rolled like a drumbeat chewing up the tracks toward North Carolina. I shut my eyes. They opened. I shut them again real tight. They opened again.

A salesman snored. I couldn't remember if he was a different man from our last stop or the one before. As passengers got off and on, they started to look like the same people over and over again. I even saw a girl who looked enough like me to be Ociee Nash. But I was me.

I listened to a boy's mother trying to quiet him. "Now, Young Bob, settle on down, you hear, or your father's going to learn of your horrendous behavior."

"Mother, I just need to cross over to look out the other side, one more time," He pleaded.

"Bobby!"

"Robert James."

"Yes, Ma'am."

Another Ben Nash in the making.

Mr. Charles would pass by me ever so often. One time he pulled Mama's quilt around my shoulders and patted my head. "Sleep well, little Ociee," he whispered. Papa would be pleased when he heard about the good care Mr. Charles was taking of me.

As tired as I was, I couldn't manage to stay asleep. All I could do was stir around in my seat.

I had never before been in one single spot for such a long time. At home there was always something that needed doing or someone, Ben most always, who was calling me to play—down by the pond or up in a tree or out at the barn. Dratted old train. I turned and stretched out my legs all the way nearly sticking out through the armrest into the aisle.

I began to study Mama's quilt. Mama called it a "log cabin" pattern because the little rectangles fitted together to form squares that got bigger and bigger. It took her one whole winter to sew it all together. During that time, she often took me and Ben with her to quilt with her lady friends. We were allowed to play with other neighbor children while all the mothers worked on one another's quilts.

Papa teased her, "Sweet wife of mine, you ladies call it a 'quilting bee,' but we men folk think it's more of a 'chatting bee.'"

I remember one time when me and Ben got into a terrible peck of trouble. Mama had one of her prize quilts sunning outside on the clothesline to freshen the smell of mothballs. Ben came and got me.

"Ociee, doesn't it sorta look like a fort to you? We could duck inside and see," he said pulling me over to the clothesline. "Can't do any harm."

"Oh, Ben, I don't know." To tell the honest truth, I knew the minute he opened his mouth we were headed for trouble, but I followed him anyway. The next thing I knew, we were both under the clothesline with Mama's quilt pushed out with big sticks held with rocks. I had a pot from the kitchen, a big spoon and my doll. Ben had his carved wood gun. We were both pretending to fight off wolves or maybe bandits, I forget which.

In the middle of the battle, Mama spotted us. She ran outside, but not to help us fight. She was mad as could be. Mama fussed, "Ben Nash, you get out from under there with your little sister. You two will surely dirty up my fine freshened quilt."

Ben pleaded, "But, Mama, you said this is a log cabin quilt so I figured it's a perfect house for Ociee and me." I couldn't help but giggle.

Mama frowned and wiped her hands on her apron. "Benjamin Nash, Josephine Nash," she said. "I have more to do than to be tricked by the likes of you. Ben, don't you be putting notions in your little sister's head."

Ben moved his lips like he was saying every word Mama said, but she didn't see him.

I covered my mouth so I wouldn't be tempted to tell on him and make things all the worse.

Mama couldn't stay angry at us for too long 'cause that was just Mama. Instead of scolding us, she sat us down under the tree and taught us what she called "the treasure" of her quilts. She said, "Now sit still, you two, and listen carefully for this is very important. Once you understand the specialness of what makes up this kind of art, you will know to treat it with the same respect you treat God's creatures, or the land around us, or even each other."

Ben smirked at me. I stuck out my tongue. Mama put her finger to her lips. She knew we were listening.

Pointing to a blue rectangle, she said in her tender voice, "That came from scrapes of Fred's baby dress. I remember the first time I took him to town to show him off, I dressed him in it." Ben thought it was so funny that his big manly brother wore a dress.

Mama said, "So did you, Ben. And you were a darling in yours. Here, here is a piece of yours, see the tiny yellow flowers?"

"Humph," Ben sniffed. Actually, he was glad to hear how cute he was, too. Ben's favorite subject was always BEN.

Mama continued, "And this one here was my old apron, remember? I think I tore it to shreds picking blackberries in it. Never did get the berry stains to bleach out. Here's a red checked piece from our table skirt."

I remembered that summer day as I fingered the quilt that now comforted me on the train. I could almost feel her touch on the spots where she had worked so diligently. Just like Papa's fingers on my strawberry sandwiches. I could see each perfect tiny white stitch Mama had made.

Mama sighed and showed me, "And look, Ociee, your Sunday dress from when you were five. And a sample from your Aunt Mamie's peach print party dress."

"Mama," I said, "Here's my dollie's coat."

"Ah," fretted Ben, "Doll's clothes, goat's nose. Quilts are still better at being forts."

The train jerked and I realized I was back in the middle of Tennessee. I sighed. The train roared on. I must remember to show Aunt Mamie the square of her party dress. I'd tell her everything I knew. I hoped that she would remember some, too. Aunt Mamie mentioned once in a letter about how she and Mama mailed parcels filled with swatches of fabric back and forth to each other. Papa had scolded Mama about paying good money to mail rags, but he wasn't truly angry. Papa never ever was mad at Mama.

I wondered if our mail car was carrying pieces of baby clothes and ladies' dresses for some other lady's family. Anyway, I knew Aunt Mamie would be happy to talk about Mama's quilt. We'd surely have plenty of time to catch up once I got to Asheville.

The salesman snored.

The boy and his mother rested.

I yawned and closed my eyes and drifted into the patterns of the quilt as I listened to the hum of the train. Aunt Mamie would be glad to talk about Mama's quilt, about girlish things. I'll show her Mama's smiling picture, too. I put my fingers on my locket and slept.

13

"Wake up, Ociee!" the voice urged.

"Aunt Mamie?" I shook my head.

"Ociee, Ociee Nash, open up those eyes of yours," said the voice. It was the voice of a man.

"Papa!"

"No, dear girl, it's Mr. Charles."

I tried to focus as I wiped the sleepy away from my eyes. The train's motion, even after almost a whole day of it, seemed unnatural. I stretched and pulled the hair back from my face. Looking outside I said, "Oh my gracious goodness, it's almost light! What time is it, Mr. Charles?"

"It's morning, but not by much. I woke you up because I couldn't let you miss this magnificient sight," he said. "Take a gander."

I couldn't believe what was looming outside the train's window. Like an enormous monster swelling up and out from the land, appeared the very first mountain I had ever seen. I was thunderstruck.

"There, Ociee Nash, is Lookout Mountain. We're almost to Chattanooga," he announced.

Our cock-a-doodle rooster couldn't have waked me quicker if he'd flown up and pecked me on my nose.

"Mr. Charles, it's the hugest thing I ever saw," I *tried* to talk quiet like, but it was mighty hard. I whispered, "Why, next to Lookout Mountain, this train is as little as a baby caterpillar crawling beside our barn."

He grinned from one ear to the other. I could see all his teeth. He had one gold tooth in the way back part of his mouth. "So you're not fussy that I got you up a little early, Ociee?"

"No sir, Mr. Charles, I'd be kicking my sleepy self if I had *missed* such a sight. I thank you for waking me."

We both watched out my window at the mountain.

"It goes on as far as I can see. Mr. Charles, when will we start our climb up over to the other side?" I asked.

He clasped his hands together and shook his head, "Oh my, no, my dear young lady," he explained almost, but not quite, laughing at me. "This train couldn't make a climb like that. I'm not making fun of you. It's just that you must have a lot more faith in this train's strength than she rates!"

"She? Is the train a girl, Mr. Charles?"

"Trains, boats, buggies, they're all girls to me, Ociee. Can't say that I know why. She's a girl, that's all."

"I guess I'll have to ponder that," I said. "I just wish *she* were headed up that old mountain with us aboard."

"I do, too, Ociee, it would be quite a trip," he exclaimed.

Mr. Charles got kind of quiet for a minute. Then he asked me if I knew much about the War between the States. I said I had heard lots of stories when the men folks would get to talking about it with Papa from time to time. Afterwards, Papa always told us the men in Mississippi seemed to get a little closer to victory with every telling.

"That I know to be true, Ociee, I expect most men who fought so hard all had to feel some sort of triumph in the War," said Mr. Charles, "It might interest you to know that a battle took place just over on the northwest side of the mountain there." He pointed out the window.

"Right over there? Oh my goodness."

"Yes, ma'am, called it the 'Battle above the Clouds,' they did. Forces under General Sherman fought the Confederates in three days of one of the bloodiest fights in the War. I lost my Uncle Daniel up there."

"I'm sorry, Mr. Charles, I'm so sorry that happened to your people."

"Why thank you, Ociee. It's been more than three decades, family's gotten accustomed to Daniel's being gone by now," he said.

"I don't understand how time can fix much of anything," I thought out loud.

"You will, Ociee. That you will learn for yourself," he said.

"Do you really think so, Mr. Charles?" I asked.

"Most certainly," he assured me. "I know that as sure as I know you'll climb to the top of that mountain one of these days. That's a fact."

"Mr. Charles, you didn't say I'd climb '*her*.' Lookout Mountain must not be a girl then?"

Mr. Charles chuckled, "Well, let me think a minute. A mountain is male all right, a craggy old man, don't you imagine?"

"A grumpy, bumpy craggy old man," I chanted.

He laughed at me.

"And one of these days, I'll climb to the top of that mountain and crawl all the way out to the end of his big gray nose. Then, when your train roars by, I'll shout, 'Hello, Mr. Charles!'"

"And I will reply, 'Good day, Miss Ociee Nash!'" he said.

He gestured outside again, "For now you can enjoy the view and keep thinking about your journey ahead. In fact, one of your adventures will begin soon. We'll arrive in Chattanooga in fifteen minutes and you'll need to get organized to change to the next train."

I swallowed real hard.

He took out his pocket watch and checked the time. He said, "Yes, fifteen minutes. We should be right on time. Ociee, I assume your father told you what you were to do once we arrive?"

I couldn't remember a thing Papa had explained to me, but I bragged in the bravest voice I could gather, "Oh, yes, I know exactly what I am to do,"

"Well, I know that; however, will you please allow me to walk you to the Asheville bound. I'd like to see you off, if you don't mind?" he asked.

I was so glad to hear that, all the air nearly left my chest. Real ladylike I said, "Well, yes sir, I'll do that for you."

That will be another good thing to tell Papa in my letter.

I gazed out at Lookout Mountain. It was an odd kind of connection with Mr. Charles and me when he said he had lost his uncle on that mountain. Did everybody's family have sorrowful times? I wanted to ask how long it took him not to be sad about his Uncle Daniel, but I didn't. I knew he was fine about it that day, and that was good to know.

He stood up and told me it was time for him to get to work. He said, "Now you just keep on studying that old man mountain there. I'll be busy running between these passenger cars for a time here." With that, Mr. Charles walked away toward the front of our train.

The mountain was out one window, and the mighty Tennessee River, more houses, churches and stores came into my view out the other window.

On the Tennessee River, I counted two ferry boats, one paddle wheeler and three tugs pushing barges which were piled high with barrels and wooden crates. It was like one of my picture books, all of a sudden, just came to life in front of me! I wished for Ben. How he would love all these sights. I felt happy and sad at the same time.

I saw people fishing in rowboats, and on the banks of the river a fat man was going in for a swim. I thought to myself that he looked like a big old cow wading in to take himself a dip.

Fred had told me about seeing the Mississippi River when he went to Memphis, but the Tennessee River was the most water I had ever seen in person. Chattanooga stretched out farther than if Abbeville and Holly Springs were lined up together. I could see nothing that looked much like a farm to me. Mostly, I saw houses and stores jammed close together sometimes touching one another. Some buildings were two stories or even three, I think. Some were made of wood, others were made from gray stone and orange red brick. We chugged into the train station. I tied on my new hat, real tight.

Mr. Charles announced, "Ladies and gentleman, we have arrived at our destination. Welcome to Chattanooga, Tennessee." He motioned me off the train and directed me to sit on a big iron bench. I was to wait right there for him. I *meant* to. My feet didn't quite reach the brick pavement under the seat. They dangled. I swung them back and forth. My locket secure, I clutched my basket, the quilt, and, especially my tag:

Ociee Nash, Asheville, North Carolina.

Hot as it was that day, I was almost frozen with fear. I'd fiddle first with the bow on my hat and next the locket, then back to the bow. Never had I seen so many people in one place. The station was a big stone building. It reminded me of the mountain, but the station had more angles than curves and it didn't have any trees. Worst of all, the station had noise and dirt and way too many people. Ladies in dresses shuffled about holding children's hands. I longed for a mama's hand. Fancy gentlemen wearing coats rushed about carrying suit cases. Most of them looked alike with their neatly trimmed mustaches.

I saw a farmer in overalls. Oh, how I longed for Papa and the boys and familiar things. Mainly, I kept my eyes in the direction of Mr. Charles and thought about how relieved I'd be once I got to my seat and was on my way to Asheville.

Then, from the far end of the station I heard the strains of the oddest kind of music. Turning to concentrate on the sound, I was shocked to see the back of a large man with curly dark hair. My heart pounded. It was him! The gypsy must have followed me all the way to Chattanooga.

I jumped from the bench. He was about as far away from me as Papa's tool shed was from the back porch. I raced toward him. The big crowds of traveling people got in my way.

"Excuse me," I said.

71

Brushing past the fancy ladies, who were walking too slow, past the businessmen, who were hard to pass because they walked too fast, past the farmers. The noisy busy people formed walls to hold me back. I spoke up, "Oh, please let me pass, please!" I broke through and finally got to where the crowd was surrounding him.

His back was to me. He hadn't seen me yet.

I could see he wore a fancy shirt. It was bright yellow with big puffed sleeves that billowed out from his brown leather vest. On his head was a small black hat with shiny purple trim.

"It's me, it's Miss Lady," I shouted to get his attention.

He turned around. He smiled at me.

"You're not *my* gypsy!" I exclaimed.

He leaned over toward me. He said, "I'm sorry to disappoint you, madam. Perhaps, you will like my little friend a bit better."

He opened the door of a red wooden box which had bars on each end. Out sprang a tiny furry animal squealing and leaping about with all its might, "Chipppeee, chipeee." Dressed in every detail that matched the man's costume, it was a real live monkey. "Yippee," I shouted.

A girl next to me clapped and jumped with me, "Look, Mommie, come and see the organ grinder's monkey."

The man played a tune on what he told us was a "hurdy-gurdy." His music made me think of circus sounds with county fair noises stirred in together. The crowd grew bigger and bigger. The organ grinder sang and laughed and played his music. His monkey danced around and shook folks' hands. I, of course, stuck out mine. Wonderful. He gripped me strong with his long, baby-sized fingers. He held my two biggest fingers really tight. His hand felt slick and soft. I could tell he had never pulled weeds or washed dishes.

I squatted down and looked him right in the eye. "Hello, monkey man."

I half expected him to say, "Hello, Miss Nash." But he didn't say a word. That monkey passed among the crowd holding out a tin can rattling with coins inside. It was clear he wanted money.

Fred sometimes passed the collection plate at church on Sundays and I saw the same look on the monkey's face. Some folks put their pennies in the can. Not me.

"Ociee, come on now," Mr. Charles called to me.

"Oh dear," I said, "I'm coming." I raced for his outstretched hand.

"I figured that monkey and his master might just get your attention, Ociee," he said. "I see them 'most every trip. You do have curiosity about this old world. You keep that up, you hear? It's a gift, that curiosity of yours is a gift."

"Yes, sir, I promise to try," I assured him.

As we walked quickly between the trains, I was glad Mr. Charles was by my side. He was walking tall in his black conductor's uniform tipping his hat to ladies along the way. He told me he had arranged for a porter to carry my trunk to the next train. I felt like a princess from a fairy tale in the company of Mr. Charles. He was like a tall soldier escorting me through the railroad yard.

The train engines made me think of a field of sleeping dragons. Smoke clung heavy in the air making my nose itch.

Whistles blasted.

Engines growled.

A real monkey, I just couldn't believe I shook hands with a real monkey.

We got to the train. "Here you are, Ociee," said Mr. Charles. "This will take you all the way to Asheville." Checking his watch piece, he said, "You should arrive easily on time."

Mr. Charles took me to the steps. "Your Papa mustn't worry a minute about the likes of you, Ociee Nash. Farewell! It has been my great pleasure to assist such a charming young girl."

"Thank you, Mr. Charles. And good-bye to you."

14

Walking down the aisle, I chose another seat by a new window. Train traveling was starting to feel more familiar to me by then. I settled into a seat that had a scratchy velvet cover an ugly color of maroon. It made me long for the sticky leather of Mr. Charles' train. Or, even better, cheerful flowered cotton cushions, or grass and hay and more normal things to touch. As we pulled out of the station, I slid open the window, leaned out and waved good-bye once again. Mr. Charles waved back, but it wasn't sad, not sad at all.

We were soon out of Chattanooga. My journey was going faster and faster now that Asheville was so much closer. I was thinking less about being lonesome and more about getting there. The new conductor announced that we were nearing Hiwassee Lake in the foothills of the Blue Ridge Mountains.

I tried to talk with him, but he wasn't a friendly sort like Mr. Charles. "I'm traveling all by myself to my Aunt Mamie's in Asheville, North Carolina."

"That's nice," he said as he hustled by.

"I've been traveling near about twenty-four hours now," I announced the next time he hurried up the aisle.

"Long time, Miss," he commented.

I found the mountains out the window far more interesting than that conductor. Besides, I wasn't feeling like I needed so much talking now. I wanted to think of Mama and Papa anyway. I was on the way to their first home, and I was almost there.

Mama and Papa often entertained us with stories about the beautiful blue mountains and how Asheville seemed destined to exist. "It is an ideal spot for people to bloom," Mama shared about romping through the dazzling wild flowers of spring, while Papa told how to build snowmen in the winter. They talked of playing on the banks of the French Broad River watching ferry boats carry folks, of making leaf collections with the spectrum of fall colors in the hardwood trees and playing year round in the green rolling hills near their homes.

Some evenings outside on our porch, Mama would talk about her home town with such a dreamy look on her face that Papa would say, "Children, your Mama's just about to rise up out of her seat and float straight away up into the clouds."

Mama always stopped him and would say, "Now George Nash, don't you forget for one minute that our farm is far more beautiful to me than any place in the whole world because we all are here together." Oftentimes, Fred would chime in and say with Mama, "Mississippi is where I've been planted. It's where I am happy with my handsome husband." Papa would walk across the porch and give her a kiss.

Someday, I decided, I'd marry someone just like Papa. Ben, on the other hand, didn't understand anything about real life. It's a mystery to me how boys turn into grown men.

I looked out at those mountains and knew that Mama's heaven would have to have mountains like those. Her mountains would make up for us all not being there with her.

I started thinking there must be some of Mama in me because I was feeling a kind of welcome from those tall mountains, the Blue Ridge.

A lady sat behind me. I turned around and rested my chin on my hand and said, "Hello."

"And hello to you, my dear," she smiled back at me.

"I'm Ociee Nash," I said showing her my tag.

"I don't have such an important paper with me," she said, as she introduced herself, "but I can tell you that I'm Miss Evelyn Baker and I'm delighted to make your acquaintance."

"Did you expect the Blue Ridge Mountains to be blue?" I asked my new traveling companion.

"Well, Ociee, I do see these lovely mountains as quite blue oftentimes," she stated. "It really depends on the time of day and the placement of the sun. Sometimes these hills and mountains glimmer as if they are made of silver, other times as I travel, they seem to be a rich and deep gray-green or even as black as pitch tar."

"Do you travel on trains a lot of times, Miss Baker?" I asked.

"Whenever opportunity presents itself, I do love a journey. And you?"

I adjusted my hat and said, "I do love a journey, too. Truth is I love *this journey*, it's my first. Miss Baker, are all trips real special?"

"Yes, my dear, I think so. But surely your very first one would be the most special of all. My late mother would have told you that you have selected the most perfect destination of all for a train trip."

"Your 'late mother,' why is your mother late, Miss Baker?" I asked.

"Oh, dear heart, *late* refers to the fact that Mother has passed on. My mother died several years ago."

"How terrible," I said.

"Thank you, Ociee, but please understand that I know that much of what my Mother was, when she was alive, still lives on in these very mountains.

"I don't understand."

"Mother always told me the birds were the spirits of all the people who had ever dwelt here in the peaks and valleys in the Carolinas."

"Birds, Miss Baker? What kind of bird do you think your mother is?"

She said, "What a charming question you have raised. Hmmm, a bluebird, I should think. Yes, a lovely blue color, bright and cheery and quite particular where she might live!"

"She sounds nice, your mother, the bluebird," I said.

"Oh, yes, indeed she was. I would imagine she would be enjoying this chat with you, dear child, as much as I."

"I like talking to you, too," I smiled. I looked at her and begged her pardon saying, "Miss Baker, I am a bit hungry, and I don't have enough to share."

"How polite you are. Do go right ahead," she said. "My, but I have enjoyed you, Ociee, Ociee Nash. A bluebird, what a delightful girl you are."

"Thank you, Miss Baker." I turned back around to eat.

Talking to Miss Baker and Mr. Charles had been almost as much fun as playing with Ben, but I wouldn't be writing him about that. He would be real mad, in fact, he'd be jealous, plain and simple.

I couldn't think of what kind of bird my Mama might be. I'd talk to Aunt Mamie about that question. I knew Papa would choose to be an eagle. I could see him swooping in and out of the sky. Papa would land on a tree on the tiptop of the very tallest mountain so he could see farther than all the other eagle fathers.

I unwrapped my last sandwich. It was cheese. Drat that Ben, he had to go and eat the cookies that Miss May baked. I was glad Papa insisted on baking another batch. Actually, I thought that Papa's were every bit as good as Miss May's. I wouldn't have the heart to tell her any more than I could brag to Ben about my train friends. I worried about hurting folks.

Tasting each crumb of the last cookie, I felt I was saying good-bye again. "I love you, Papa."

Smoke again puffed past my opened window. Lands sake! I must be dirty as pitch. My white hankie had turned nearly black with my trying to stay clean. I hoped Aunt Mamie wouldn't mind. Of course she wouldn't, after all, she is an experienced traveler like me.

Aunt Mamie, I thought to myself, I know you sew real well. I remember that you are a good cook, too, aren't you? No worry if you aren't, though. I'll teach you. I would be very helpful to Aunt Mamie in every way. Papa said I should. I know you love me, I added, hoping.

The mountains were getting taller and taller. I tried to imagine how my parents must have dreamed more than eighteen years ago, as they looked out at the very spot I was seeing right then. Before there was me, before Fred and Ben, Mama and Papa passed these same big, blue mountains for their last look as they headed west to settle our farm.

I knew Papa wasn't scared, not Papa. There he was, young and handsome and brand-new married, riding a train on his way out west to become a Mississippi farmer. Papa did anything he set his mind to do. We all honored that about him.

But I wondered, was Mama's heart beating fast like mine was that minute? I could put my hand on my chest and feel the *boom, boom, boom* that matched the *chug, chug, chug* of the train's wheels on the steel tracks. Was it hard for her to leave *her* people, and *her* home, and *her* things, *her* familiar sounds and smells, *her* quiet places?

I was sure that Mama and Papa must have seen the very same peaks that I was looking toward. The trees, they must have been smaller then, the pines. The hardwoods grew up the mountains just so far, then they'd stop. Bald gray rocks jutted out through the shades of green like animal heads watching after our train.

I saw the rolling hills, some taller than others, some flat on top, others pointed. I saw winding roads that threaded up through the mountains and disappeared to who knows where. Mama and Papa might have wondered, as I did that day. Where were the people, or the Indians, or soldiers, or bears? Those mountains must hold so many secrets.

Mama, what kind of bird are you? Are you a wren? Do you land on ladies' knitting baskets and select bright threads to decorate your nest? Is your nest filled with the softest hay and the strongest pine straw for your babies?

I unfolded the red scarf in Miss May's basket and took out the painting of Mama.

I'm going home in your and Papa's place, Mama.

I was ready to get there for her, for Papa, and for me. Once again, in the quiet of late morning, I fell asleep holding Mama's picture.

15

I must have been more worn out than I thought. I was a bit aware of someone touching my tag, but for the next few hours I mainly slept. When we reached Hazelwood, Miss Baker tapped my hand and said good-bye, but I hardly noticed she was leaving.

Before I realized it, the conductor shook my shoulder and said, "Ociee Nash, you must to get off the train now. Miss Nash, we are in Asheville. We have arrived at your destination."

Like a raccoon when Fred fires his gun in the air, I jumped up and scurried for the exit. I forgot everything. I stopped, hurried back to my seat. I stuck my hat on, backwards, I think, grabbed my things, and nearly fell down the steps onto the train platform.

I searched for Aunt Mamie. She was nowhere to be seen. The station was full—full of traveling men, ladies, and children. But there were no aunts, not *my* aunt, anyway. Everyone seemed paired up or, at least, pretty certain of what they were doing. Some left the station. Some got back on the train. I stood there all by myself, not at all sure what to do.

I said to me, "All right, Ociee, just get yourself freshened up before Aunt Mamie sees you. This will work out better because you'll have extra time to get presentable."

I found the wash room quickly, soaped up my hands and face and splashed the warm fresh water. Drying myself, I had to admit, I did most definitely feel better. Clean and fresh, hat adjusted, tag showing, I took a deep breath and walked back out into the station quite certain I'd see my aunt.

"All Aboard!" The whistle shrieked. The engine started up, "chug, chug, chug." Suddenly, I got scared. I rushed to the ticket man and asked, "Sir, this is Asheville, North Carolina, isn't it?"

"Yes'm, right you are," he answered.

Another deep breath. At least, I had gotten off in the right place.

I was glad this station wasn't as crowded with people coming and going like Chattanooga. But I *was* hoping for one person, for Aunt Mamie. Where could she be? Maybe she changed her mind about me. Maybe she never wanted me in the first place. Or she got sick or her buggy turned over on the way to pick me up. Or maybe she died.

"Sir, could you tell me, please, has anybody been looking for a passenger from Abbeville, Mississippi?"

"No one has asked me that particular question, little lady. But now, if you notice this schedule and take a look over there at that big clock on the wall, you'll understand that your train pulled in a good thirty minutes early today."

I saw the clock and, sure enough, the little hand was on the twelve and the big hand was on the six. It was only 12:30.

"I'm so glad you told me that. I thought someone forgot me!"

"Of course not. Fact is, most of the time, the trains tend to run just a little late. You should sit right here and wait for your people."

I looked around for a minute and asked, "How far is 66 Charlotte Street from here?"

He replied, "Oh, that would be several blocks, Miss. What are you planning to do with that big trunk of yours? I don't recommend you tote it all the way to Charlotte Street!"

"No, I don't guess so." I said.

"Let me step out of here and call you a buggy," he offered.

"Sir, no thank you just the same. There is one thing, however; can you please direct me to where to send a telegram? I want my Papa to know that I got here all right."

"Yes, ma'am," he said, pointing to a door just a few steps ahead. "You go on over there, and I'll watch your things for you."

"Why, that's very kind, thank you," I said.

I walked through the door of the telegraph office. Very much like the Abbeville office, it had a writing table, a counter and a man who sat at a desk near the message machine. He wore a black hat without a middle in it. His blond hair stuck up and out like bird feathers. He got up and came over to me.

"Afternoon, Miss, help you?"

"Yes, you may," I said.

I gave him our address, I did just like Papa. I wrote in pencil:

Arrived Asheville STOP
Am fine STOP
Shook monkey's hand STOP
Love Ociee STOP

I opened my coin purse and counted out 50 cents to pay for my telegram. "Let's see, four, five, six cents, a dime, a twenty-five cent piece, three nickels and my silver dollar. That should be plenty enough, just in case," I assured myself.

I walked back to the front of the train station and searched the platform again. Still no Aunt Mamie.

The man came back out of his ticket booth. He said, "All set, Miss?"

"Yes, thank you."

"I'll call that buggy for you now," he said.

"No. Thank you anyway, sir; I can do that myself."

I dragged my trunk out to the walk and placed my basket and the quilt on top. I waved at a fine fancy buggy that had the word "cab" printed on the door.

"Whoa."

The driver jumped down from his seat and, as I watched him carefully, he loaded everything into the back. He then took my hand and helped me up into the passenger section. I felt like a sure enough princess then.

"Where to, Ma'am?"

"Take me to 66 Charlotte Street, please."

"Giddy up, Old Horse," said the driver clicking his tongue.

81

We rumbled down the road for just a few minutes when we pulled up in front of Aunt Mamie's house.

I made it! I really and truly made it! *66 Charlotte Street, Asheville, North Carolina.* I had read that address on the corner of envelopes from Aunt Mamie's house ever since I had learned to read. I had written to that address as soon as I learned to write. Papa had lived there. Mama had lived there. Now, it was my turn.

The front door of the white two-story house opened. I saw the back of a lady, she was calling inside, "I'm leaving now to pick up my darling little Ociee at the station. Please watch out for our turkey roast. Can't be burning up her welcome dinner. Oh, I see the buggy we sent for has already arrived for me."

The lady turned. It was Aunt Mamie. And she had on her traveling hat, too. Hers had big red roses all across the brim.

As she walked toward the cab. I jumped out from inside. The driver winked at me and announced, "I have a young lady looking for 66 Charlotte Street."

Aunt Mamie screamed, "Gracious, goodness, sakes alive!" as she hurried toward me with her arms outstretched.

I raced up the walkway as fast as I could. I threw myself at her. Both of our hats sailed off and landed in her front yard's fresh green grass.

"Welcome, Ociee Nash, my darling girl."

"Oh, Aunt Mamie, I am really truly here!"

We hugged a quick time and stepped back to look at one another.

I got here early, did you know, Aunt Mamie?"

"Well, dear, so I see! Were you frightened, precious girl?" she asked as she pulled me close once again. I felt that hug from the top of my head down to the bottoms of my feet.

It was a real, true, family kind of hug. As we hung on to each other, I smelled the scent of her lavender soap and melted into the warmth of her arms. We stood there wrapped around each other for a mighty long while.

I remembered her question. Cradled under her chin, I answered, "No, not me, Aunt Mamie, I wasn't frightened, not for one single minute."

Aunt Mamie kept me close and signaled the driver. She said, "Excuse our delay, it's just that I have hoped for this moment for a very long time. She sighed. "Oh, but course, we are to pay her fare."

I quickly chimed in insisting, "Please, Aunt Mamie, I can take care of this."

"Very well, Ociee," she said with a smile.

I opened my coin purse and emptied all the contents into the driver's hands. I said, "Here, please take it all. I don't want to think about Papa's money another minute. Besides, this was my first cab ride ever, and it was worth every penny to me."

"Why, young lady," he said, keeping only the dime, "put your money back for another day. The pleasure was all mine anyway. I think I will use your fare to buy sugar for this horse of mine. Would you approve of that?"

"Yes, sir!"

The driver turned his buggy as he waved good-bye to us, "Enjoy yourselves, ladies."

"We intend to do just that," said Aunt Mamie. "And thank you again."

Turning to me, my aunt asked, "Are you hungry, Ociee?"

I replied, "About as hungry as that horse is for his sugar!"

"I have a special dinner all planned for you. Let's go inside, Ociee Nash," she said taking my hand in hers.

"I would like that, Aunt Mamie."

As we made our way up the brick path toward the front porch, I reached down and picked up both of our hats. We walked into the house, I wore Aunt Mamie's and she wore mine.

Part Two

Papa, Ociee, and Ben.
(Courtesy of CineVita Productions)

Mr. Charles with Ociee
(Courtesy of CineVita Productions)

Aunt Mamie
(Courtesy of CineVita Productions)

16

Aunt Mamie was chubby. There was no denying it. She was the kind of chubby that made her good at hugging folks. She was especially good at hugging me. And she was a grand cook. I knew that as soon as I tasted the first bite of her *Welcome Ociee to Asheville Feast*. With her turkey roast, we had fried corn and green beans, candied sweet potatoes, biscuits, and chocolate cake for dessert. That was three weeks and two days ago today.

I was really very fortunate to be living in Asheville with an aunt who was such a good cook. Aunt Mamie was also smart. She could spell any word a person tested her with without having to pull out the dictionary.

I shouldn't have been homesick, not for one single minute, given all the attention she was paying me. My spelling was already greatly improved, too.

Oh yes, and she was teaching me all kinds of things, things I loved, such as how to fix fancy flowers for the dining room table. That naturally led to her showing me how to repair her very expensive vases when I dropped them.

"Unimportant companions to creating," she termed broken flower containers, or spilled water on her fine wood furniture, or the other fruits of my learning. "Fruits" was her wonderful way of saying messes.

But even my dear aunt couldn't replace the good things about the home I had known all my whole life.

There, I said it.

———————

Aunt Mamie was the only cheery thought I had as I stretched my lonesome self up into the still unfamiliar bed. Act like the big girl you are, Ociee, I would say as I said my prayers. Then, by the time I God blessed Papa, and Aunt Mamie, Fred and Ben, I'd be crying. I'd look at Mama's picture, the one my gypsy painted, and pledge to feel as much at home there as Mama once did. The next day, I'd make my silly self smile, so my aunt wouldn't know.

The emptiness of everything was still missing Mama, and that Papa and my brothers were a forever twenty-nine hour train ride away from me. And I missed Rebecca something terrible. Papa said he'd like to bring her to me for a visit, but trains had very strict rules about traveling with calves. Papa checked and Mr. Hall said, "Even for Miss Ociee, there can be no exception." He said he was sorry. He couldn't have been all that sorry or he would have found a way.

I pulled the sheet up around my neck. Never had thought much about the lumps in my own bed in Mississippi until I tried to settle into the smooth one in North Carolina. As long as I could remember, I'd cuddled between those lumps. They knew to cradle me just right. During my first long nights in Asheville, lying on that smooth bed, I'd curl up tight in Mama's quilt and wish for the everyday things of home in Mississippi.

My head kept telling me I was in my new home with Aunt Mamie on Charlotte Street. Most of the rest of me longed to be back on our farm. As much as I loved my aunt, my heart was confused as to where I truly belonged.

Since Mama died, almost everything had been turned upside down and backwards for me. But like Papa said over and over again, I was trying to make the best of things.

Tomorrow would be another day.

I was going to a school in Asheville, but it was Aunt Mamie who was teaching me the most. She was training me to be a real lady. We had tea together every day around 4:00 o'clock. I enjoyed the cookies. I was getting to where I didn't spill too much stirring the sugar into our tea cups. I also had to practice my patience before tea time because we sometimes ran late if one of our customers stayed longer than we expected. My aunt was truly a fine seamstress, just like Papa had said. She fashioned dresses, skirts and blouses and hats for the ladies of Asheville. I liked it when the ladies came in to be fitted and bragged so about her work.

I helped. Actually, I was learning to help, which meant I experienced a few more of my aunt's "unimportant companions to creating." I had a problem attaching collars backwards instead of frontwards. I managed to sew buttons to button holes. And once I took out a bodice so many times that I left teeth holes right where the lady's bust would go. We had to start all over with new fabric. Aunt Mamie said, "Ripping out is part of mastering one's ability, but it's best not to bite with such vigor, my darling."

I giggled, promising once again to be more careful.

I loved the smells of freshly cut cloth and the garden's scents that drifted through the opened south windows. I chirped along with Aunt Mamie's canary. I clicked my tongue to the ricky-tick of the sewing machine. The smells and sounds of our workplace were as unique to me as were the ladies' things we created with our cutting, pinning, and stitching.

One Saturday morning, to make Aunt Mamie laugh, I put thimbles on all my fingers and all my toes and made my own tap dancing music. She clapped and put a thimble on the tip of her nose. We both just laughed and laughed. I realized that my aunt was fun in the same way Mama was fun.

In the weeks that followed, I was to see sunshine in Asheville.

Aunt Mamie's house was pretty. It looked like an outside-in garden. The aroma of lavender filled the air. Every room had different flowered wallpaper, mostly roses. Yellow roses, bigger than my whole head, decorated the dining room walls. I knew they were exactly that big because, early one morning, I measured. I moved the chair away from the wall. Putting my nose in the center of a rose bloom, I closed first one eye, then the other. I could see the bloom's borders just to the left and then just to the right of each of my ears. My nose still in place, my chin touched the blossom's bottom and my hair bow ribbon touched the blossom's top.

The next room, the parlor, was covered in thousands of deep pink, thumb-size, climbing roses. Aunt Mamie even had the wall-paper man cover the ceiling with the pattern. I loved that room. It was in there we had our tea parties.

I'd lie down on the floor and look up to the tiptop of the four-teen-foot-tall ceiling and pretend I was a snail crawling about in the garden. I never played that game if a customer was due to come in. Aunt Mamie would enjoy that, but a proper lady from Asheville might think the little farm girl from Mississippi "a bit odd." I was not about to embarrass my aunt, or Papa.

In the room where I slept on that smooth bed, the paper's flowers were blue. They weren't Morning Glories or any other ordinary flower. They were magic. They were anything I wanted them to be. Some days, I'd pretend they were flowers from olden days that twined up the tower of a princess's castle. I, of course, played the princess who could lean out, when it took her fancy, and pick a magic blue posy.

Other times, I declared the flowers on my room's walls could only be found on a certain star that blinked outside my bedroom window just to the right of the oak tree. Other days, I dreamed of them growing in a field where Papa and the boys were busy planting. The blooms would burst into vegetables that even picky Ben would choose to eat.

My Aunt Mamie insisted all her wallpaper was glued on with extra sweet honey paste. "In the springtime, my dear darling Ociee, the bees will fly in and out to get their best honey from our pretty floral walls."

I wished for Spring and for those bees. I wished for Papa. Homesick was a good way to describe a person's feelings. When home is too far away, it can make even a cheerful person feel very sick. Some days, I ached through and through all the way from my eyelashes to the bottom of my stomach.

Ben, I missed Ben, and I knew he missed me. I couldn't let go of my mind's picture of Ben when the train pulled out of Abbeville. Tears washed his cheeks and all the way down his throat. Papa wrote and told me Ben cried so much he got his tie sopping wet.

When I think back about it, I cried harder the day I left on the train than I did at Mama's funeral. I pondered why that was. I finally decided I must have been plain numb at the funeral. It was kind of like cutting my finger real bad. It doesn't hurt right off, it's frozen like. Then, in a few seconds, there's a gush of blood. The awful throbbing starts. Mama's death was like that. Mama's death, Mama's death, I still can hardly believe it.

It seemed like only minutes ago.

No, it seemed like years had passed.

No, it seemed like it never happened.

And yet, it seemed like it happened again every single day.

Papa wanted to go straight to Heaven to be with Mama. He would say, over and over and over again, "But I know you need your Papa. Your Mama's watching over me and making certain I care properly for you three."

In the long, short, sad, busy, lonely, dark weeks that came afterwards, Papa tried hard. We all did.

Once I went to live in Asheville, I liked to think back to those months back home, especially of the funny things that happened. It seemed best to put the sad memories on a shelf and remember only the happy ones.

Fred would fuss so when he wrote to me, "Ben just gets in my way." But Papa would write that he didn't mind Ben's antics one bit. He liked the way Ben made him laugh. Papa told us, "Ben stirs in the merriment. And that matters, too, along with Fred's hard work. The days go by faster because of Benjamin Nash's capers. *And* Fred knows that too, deep down inside."

Last week, Papa wrote to us about how Ben got chased around the pasture and clean up the rise by an angry billy goat. Papa explained to Ben that he must have said something to the goat that set him off. It made Ben mad as could be.

"Didn't say nothing to that crazy goat," said Ben. I can just see him sitting at that table, his arms folded across his chest, acting miffed. I told Aunt Mamie that oftentimes Ben would do something dumb on purpose just to see Papa's eyes squint up with a big old grin.

Ben enjoyed being Ben. And I missed him something awful.

17

"Ociee, sweet Ociee, where are you, dearest?"

"Out here, out here swinging on the porch, Aunt Mamie," I replied. "Thought I'd catch Mr. Lynch driving by our house in his taxi buggy this pretty afternoon. I have some carrots for Old Horse."

Aunt Mamie's heels tapped on the wood floor in the hallway, and out the front door she came. She took hold of the arm of the porch swing and said, "Did you hear yourself, Ociee?"

"Yes ma'am, I said I am waiting for Mr. Lynch, thought he might let me give Old Horse a taste of these carrots here." Then I realized what was wrong and said, "Oh, I'm sorry, I should have asked you if I could do that."

"Gracious, darling girl, you can give that horse the whole bushel of carrots for that matter. After all, Old Horse pulled his buggy full of you to me!" She continued, "Dearest, do you suppose we should do something to thank Mr. Lynch? I think the two of us should prepare a basket of our best goodies for him to eat."

"Oh yes, Aunt Mamie, let's do that," I agreed.

My aunt said, "Besides, he seems taken with the likes of you. I see him wave each time he drives by."

Her face erased its smile. Aunt Mamie put her finger to her lips and said "But, Ociee, that's not what I was referring to when I came outside." She smiled again and explained, "I was meaning to ask if you heard yourself say, 'see if Mr. Lynch was to bring his buggy by *our* house'? My dear, you said '*our house*' with the same ease you usually say '*our farm*' talking about your Papa's place. I believe you really are starting to put down some roots in *your* Charlotte Street home."

"Roots, Aunt Mamie? Like tree roots, or carrot roots?" I held up the carrot. I asked, halfway giggling and half serious, "Do folks grow roots like vegetables? Do they attach themselves places?"

She joined in on my little game of words, "Well, I think the way we humans work is that we can take root in more than one spot. It takes a bit longer for a little girl to take root than it would for an ordinary old carrot, but your roots can grow deeper and in number of different spots," she said clicking her tongue. "Miss Carrot, would you like to sample a taste of gingerbread, fresh from the oven?"

"Oh, Aunt Mamie, I would indeed. I noticed that good smell all the way out here." I started to scoot forward in the swing so as to go in and help her.

She held me to the seat, "Tell you what, Ociee, you have already worked so hard in school and with me this week, why don't you just warm yourself in the afternoon sun and keep your eyes open for Mr. Lynch? I'll hurry back to the kitchen and cut you a piece of gingerbread. I'll bring it to you with a cup of apple juice. How would that do?"

"Mighty fine, ma'am!" I blurted out, almost forgetting that I was a prim and proper young lady nowadays, and not prone to squealing out so.

While she was gone, I drifted into a daydream. That was the way I got back to Mississippi for my *memory visits*. After all, I didn't want to let my roots grow too awfully deep in North Carolina.

I decided to do my dreaming about trains. Both brothers loved trains, especially freights. We had a big orchard near the train track. After the fruit got good and ripe, Fred and Ben would put some apples or peaches in a sack. Then they'd put their ears to the track and listen out for a train coming. Soon, there it would be, and they'd run like wind along side the tracks. They'd reach high and pass the sack of fruit up to the engineer, sometimes to the fireman. After awhile, those train folks would slow the train and look out for my brothers to see if they were toting fruit.

By last summer I finally got big enough to do it, too. One day a really slow train was passing. Ben and I were running along after the back end. All of a sudden, Fred picked me up and, whoosh, I got a little ride on that train. Ben did, too.

Neither one of us got hurt, but when we told Papa about our fun, it was Papa, who got hurt. He said to us real serious, he was, "Children, my heart just pains me that you get into so much mischief."

He wasn't really fussing at us. He just felt like it was his fault that he couldn't care for us as thoroughly as he wanted, not all by himself. I always figured that was one of the reasons Papa had to send me to Aunt Mamie.

At first, I only hoped my aunt truly wanted me to be with her. Then one morning, after I had gotten better settled, I had real reason to believe she liked having me there. What she said was, "Ociee, you make this house merrier every minute you're in it." Aunt Mamie had a knack of saying things that made me feel pretty good.

"Sorry it took me so long, Ociee. Miss Kitty Cat was meowing for her saucer of cream. You know how demanding she is. Why, you would think she was Mrs. George Vanderbilt up there at the Biltmore Estate, although I hardly think Mrs. Vanderbilt is anything as fussy as is our Miss Kitty. Anyway, here you are, my dear."

"Thank you, very much," I said, taking the gingerbread and the cup of apple juice very carefully. I was trying my best not to spill.

"Aunt Mamie, I was just thinking about Ben and Fred."

"Missing them, are you, dearest?"

"Yes, ma'am."

"It won't distress you quite so much in a few weeks more," encouraged Aunt Mamie. "You are still getting used to things and fighting that terrible, awful homesickness. Tincture of time, dear heart, tincture of time."

"I hope that's true, Aunt Mamie," I moaned. Then, to turn away from the sad talk, I decided to tell her another adventure about me and my brothers. "Did Papa ever write to you about Fred's runway?"

"Oh, Fred's famous runway, that he did. Your poor Papa. The good Lord gave that man an extra spot of worry in his brain, I fear. He wrote me about that runway, in great detail. Oh, dear me."

I put down my cup and plate so that I could show her with both my hands free. "Sure was tasty, thank you, Aunt Mamie." I stood up and reached way high as tall as I could. "Anyway, Fred built his runway on the tallest incline he could find. Naturally, it was mighty flat compared to the mountains around us here, Aunt Mamie. But we thought Fred's runway was something grand." I squatted down to show her just how long and wide it was, "He fashioned a cart with a old piece of pine wood and four wheel barrow wheels." I showed how Fred greased it up, "He covered the wheels real good with Papa's lard, then he rolled the cart to the top and let it go."

I sucked in a big gasp of air and kept on talking. "First, Fred let the cart run down the hill by itself a time or two. Then he took a turn. Then he sent Ben. Why, Aunt Mamie, Ben went just a whizzing! Then, guess what? It was my turn. I was the littlest, so, you guessed it, I went the fastest of all."

Aunt Mamie was patting the big white lace collar of her dress like she was trying to start up her breath. "Your guardian angels must have had their arms all around you children every single minute during those rides."

"Oh, Aunt Mamie, it was a thrill."

"It's a wonder you lived, thrill or no thrill," she said shaking her head. Aunt Mamie put down her empty tea cup and hugged me close.

95

"Aunt Mamie, I'll guess you would have gone for a runway ride, too, if you'd been there?"

"Me? Gracious no!" she said. I still believed she would.

"Now, Ociee, I will share one tiny secret with you. If you promise not to tell?"

I promised, crossed my heart and everything.

She whispered in my ear as if someone was listening, "You children take after your Papa. That's the truth of it. He was always getting into things when he was a little fellow. That's probably why he worries so about the three of you. He understands exactly how your imaginations work on mischief, that George Nash."

"Like what? Aunt Mamie, please tell me," I begged.

"Oh, he was a scoundrel of a boy, George was. Let me see. Oh! Every so often, he would hide under my bed. As soon as I blew out my light, he'd kick on the bed slats up under me and scare me to wit's end."

I laughed, "Sounds like Ben. Wonder why you never looked under the bed before you climbed in?"

"What, and ruin the fun for the both of us?"

I laughed until my stomach hurt.

Afterward, we sat quietly. Then we'd catch one another's eye and start all over again, smiling and snickering and laughing.

I liked to swing on my new front porch. When I used to swing on the porch with Papa, it was different. He and I talked, listened to the crickets, to the cows mooing, the chirps of the katydids and to the forlorn voices of whippoorwills.

There on Charlotte Street, Aunt Mamie and I talked, but there were no cows or chickens to chime in as we chatted. We heard city sounds. Neighbors' voices echoed from close-by windows. Buggies rumbled up and down our street day and night. Folks came and went by foot, some on cycles, others rode horses. Every chance I got, I'd sit on the front steps to watch the ongoing parade of city sights.

Sometimes, a passerby would stop to chat. A lady might smile and ask about my aunt and then, when I'd been there a while, she might ask about me. I knew soon to say, "Thank you, I'm fine today, how about you?" Aunt Mamie was right, my roots were beginning to sprout in Asheville. Being there was beginning to feel normal.

A gentleman would occasionally tip his hat to us. I'd smile nicely back at him. A girl or boy or my most special friend, Elizabeth Murphy, might turn up our walk and invite me to play. With Aunt Mamie's permission, I would accept if we weren't too busy with the sewing. That was fun, and Aunt Mamie always, I mean *always*, offered cookies or other special goodies for us to share. She did so especially if it was Elizabeth or if she was friends with the child's family, or even more so if the child's mama was one of her sewing customers. Her customers were very important to our livelihood. I was not sure what *livelihood* was, but I knew that mattered.

"Ociee, Ociee Nash," I heard Mr. Lynch calling to me from three houses down.

He stopped in front of our house. "Whooaah, Old Horse."

I bolted down the front steps and out into the street. "Mr. Lynch, I've been waiting for you and Old Horse all this afternoon long. Look and see what I have." With that, I produced the carrots. "Can I feed them to him, Mr. Lynch? Please, *may* I, I meant to say?"

"Of course, you may, Ociee."

"I don't know about most buggy horses, Mr. Lynch, but Old Horse here, seems to have a special fondness for my carrots."

Mr. Lynch teased me, he said, "I can't help but think yours must be tastier than any in town. Now, how can we repay you for such a nice treat? Hmmm, let's just see here," Mr. Lynch said, as he put his hand to his temple and thought real hard.

Old Horse licked his lower lip and looked at me as if to say, "Another carrot, please."

Mr. Lynch said, "I got an idea, Ociee, go in and see if you and your aunt could go for a buggy ride."

"Hooray," I hollered and ran in the house to ask.

Much to my disappointment, she said 'no.'

"But, on second thought," she observed my distress and added, "why don't you go on with Mr. Lynch? I think that would be a lovely treat for you." She opened her coin purse and giving me a nickel, walked me to the front door.

"Thank you, Aunt Mamie."

"You're welcome," she said, "And, Ociee, here's a wrap for around your shoulders so you won't take a chill." She reached for a brown knitted shawl that hung on the hall tree.

I took it and scampered out the door. Mr. Lynch helped me up onto the seat beside him, tipped his hat at my aunt, and we headed out onto Charlotte Street.

18

Asheville itself was becoming more recognizable to me. I knew neighbors in most of the houses on our block and on the two or three blocks closest to us. I knew the merchants in markets where we shopped for fresh vegetables and fruit, the ones where we went for our meat and so on.

We buggied past where Aunt Mamie bought the fabric for the ladies' clothes, at least, the fabric she didn't order special through the mail. I liked the word "fabric." It sounded foreign. "Fabric, fabric, fa-ber-ric." Aunt Mamie also bought some of her buttons and her needles, threads and other such "notions" in that store.

We passed the Post Office. That was my favorite place because we went there to mail letters home to Papa and the boys and to pick up their letters to us. Oftentimes, Papa wrote a letter to Aunt Mamie and then a separate one addressed just to me. I saved each and every one in an old candy box. Ben had even written me two times. He bragged about how much bigger he had grown since summer, but I understood what he *didn't* write about. He didn't write that he was lonely because I was in Asheville and he was all by himself with Papa and Fred in Mississippi. My thought was that it was easier to leave than to be left.

It was late in the afternoon. I was glad I had my wrap because, just like my aunt said, the chill was coming up pretty fast. Old Horse's hoofs danced down the brick street. It made me proud to sit up front next to Mr. Lynch.

I waved to my friend. "Hey, Elizabeth, look at me!" She waved back. "I gave Old Horse carrots and now he's giving me a ride. Come over tomorrow, please!"

She ran behind us waving, "Yes, yes, I'll ask Mother."

Elizabeth was my best friend, my best friend in the whole state of North Carolina. She was taller than me, real skinny, had black hair that her mama fixed all sorts of different ways; pulled into bows, pigtails, sometimes in a knot on top of her head. Her papa called us "salt and pepper" because I was blond and fair-skinned and Elizabeth was dark-headed with olive skin. "Olive skin, Elizabeth is green!" We both liked to giggle. We giggled all the time.

Old Horse clomped to a steady beat. Mr. Lynch nodded to the preacher who was posting a sign in front of our church. It read,

"Covered Dish Supper, Wednesday Nights,
Everyone's Welcomed."

"Now there's a good place to eat dessert," said Mr. Lynch, "the church women always take their best pies and cakes to those events. They like to show off their good cooking for the other women."

I smiled thinking of the times I went with Aunt Mamie. "That church food is good, Mr. Lynch, except I always take too much of everything and it tends to run together on my plate," I explained. "It turns out like a big old pile of goodness knows what. I spend all my eating time separating the beans from the peas and the potatoes from the rice."

"That's why I stick to just eating the pies at church suppers," he said.

"But that's not good for you," I tried to tell him.

"Ociee, I'm a bachelor man and I don't know much about what's good for me. I appreciate it but you mustn't be concerned. Besides, I mostly eat at my boarding house. Mrs. Lilly likely offers enough of that 'good for you' food there."

"Mr. Lynch, you'll just have to come to supper at our house," I suggested. Words had a way of tumbling out sometimes before I really thought things out. "I'll have to check with Aunt Mamie, first."

"That's mighty kind of you, Ociee. Speaking of your aunt, we don't want to worry her, I expect we should turn back in a block or so," he said.

"Oh, not so soon," I pleaded, "unless you have to pick up an important fare?"

He replied with a big grin, "Can't think of anyone more important than you. And I am very sure this horse of mine would agree."

Important. Important? I thought about Mrs. Vanderbilt, that lady Aunt Mamie had talked about. I asked him if he had ever carried her in his buggy.

"No ma'am, a lady like that has her very own transportation; buggies, horses, even one of those horseless carriages, perhaps."

"A horseless carriage, imagine!" I sighed. It was my heart's dream to have a ride in one. I'd add that to my list of things that I planned to have happen to me. I kept the list in my candy box along with letters from Papa and Ben and Fred.

Mr. Lynch popped Old Horse, "Giddup, fellow." He started talking about the Vanderbilts. "They surely have created a big stir around this part of the state. The family is real wealthy from the railroad business. Ociee, did you know they even built their own three-mile train track? "Naturally, that's small potatoes compared to the railroads the Vanderbilts have built all around this country. Anyway, their 'personal' piece of rail spurs off from the station where you came in. They use it to ship building materials and such from the station on up to their property. Their very own track, how about that?"

"My goodness." Here I had been so impressed with myself for riding on one little old train, and the Vanderbilts *owned* bunches of 'em. The world was certainly getting more amazing for me every day that passed. I asked, "So they must have a great big farm, do they Mr. Lynch?"

"You could say that! Theirs is called 'an *estate*' and people say it's nearly 125,000 acres including Mt. Pisgah itself."

"The Vanderbilts' farm sounds as big as Mississippi," I gasped. "They must have lots of children to help with all the chores."

"No, dear, in fact, there are no children. The Vanderbilts only recently married. And in Paris, France. Folks tell me Mr. Vanderbilt and his bride, Edith Stuyvesant Dresser, went all over Europe on their wedding trip."

"Gracious, goodness sakes," I shook my head. I couldn't even imagine such. "I reckon she missed her people while she was gone."

"I reckon," said Mr. Lynch. "Do you want to hear more about the house?"

"Oh yes!"

"Its something like 250 rooms including an indoor swimming pool, and forty-three bathrooms," he continued.

"A swimming pool—inside the house? Land sakes, Mr. Lynch. And forty-three bathrooms?" I sputtered out my words. I had hardly grown accustomed to having one bathroom, *inside*. That took my breath.

Mr. Lynch went on to say that beginning in 1889, they broke ground for the house and that a whole community had to be built for the hundreds of workers and craftsmen. "It took five long years of work to complete, and once finished, eighty servants work all the time simply to keep it up. Ociee, it's so fancy a home that it's even got a name. It's called the Biltmore House."

I'd heard the name before but I wanted to be silly so I said, "You don't mean it? Mr. Lynch, you reckon it's called Bilt-more, because they just keep building more and more on it?"

"You may have a good thought there, little lady, you just may have a good thought," he laughed.

I'd never heard such a thing. Even the finest homes in Holly Springs wouldn't have needed that many workers to keep things shiny clean.

Mr. Lynch mentioned that the estate kept as many as 40 horses in the stables at one time. That was surely an enormous number of horses to feed and brush and exercise. "How many carrots it would take for me to treat the Vanderbilt's horses?"

"Tell you what, Ociee, let's just say you should keep your carrot giving limited to this Old Horse," suggested Mr. Lynch. "The Vanderbilt stable would be too much for the likes of you to take on."

"Yes, sir, I agree."

We had turned a full circle around the neighborhood and, before long, we were back in front of Aunt Mamie's at 66 Charlotte Street.

"I can't thank you enough for taking me, Mr. Lynch," I moved to jump off the wagon."

"Whoa there, girl. Let me help you down from here."

"No, thank you, sir," I said as I jumped safely to the walkway. "Don't you be forgetting, I'm a farm girl. Why I've been hopping off wagons all my life. I gotta keep in practice for when I go home."

Going around to the front of the buggy, I patted the horse's soft nose, "Thank you, too, Old Horse. It was a wonderful, smooth ride."

"We enjoyed you, Ociee. See you soon. "

He was off in a second. I know he must have had a fare waiting, but I was glad he rode me first.

I hurried inside.

"Aunt Mamie, we must come up with a name for our house."

19

Clang, clang, clang! The frightful, harsh fire bell shook the night. Clang, clang! It was pitch dark. And cold. At first, too afraid to move a single toe, I curled up tighter in my covers.

"Fire!" Voices from outside screamed, "Fire, fire!"

Was it us? Was it our home? The voices yelled from every direction. I had to move. I jumped from the safeness of Mama's quilt. Breath. I touched Mama's locket. It was safe and, right then, so was I. My heart pounded.

Aunt Mamie's slippered feet scurried down the hall.

I met her and grabbed her close. "What is it, what is it, Aunt Mamie?" I screamed. I was shaking all over.

"Ociee, I don't know yet, let's hurry to the window."

As we peered out, the streets were full as the middle of the day. I saw people, mostly men, running in their night clothes. There was tremendous noise and confusion. Anxiety marked the faces of people who passed close to our porch's light. Aunt Mamie, her arms tight around me, said, "Hear the sound of the bell atop the water wagon? Listen. All the noise seems to be coming from that direction," she said, pointing down south towards where Mr. Lynch and I had buggied that very afternoon.

I looked, but all I could make out was a flood of people moving fast. Some carried lanterns. Some toted buckets. We could smell smoke. Voices shouted, "Fire." Voices shrieked, "Charlotte Street." I heard, "Hurry, this way!" I felt the clanging of the bell deep into my bones. A fire! A fire could be a giant. And that giant, that monster was gobbling up something close to me. It was somewhere near our house, our neighborhood. I was terror stricken. Everyone, the voices of everyone outside my window, sounded as frightened as was I.

We saw our neighbor as he scrambled out onto his front porch. Mr. McCall belonged to Asheville's volunteer fire brigade. I remember that Aunt Mamie once told me that it made her feel safer having a fireman next door. That night having a fireman next door didn't make me feel safe. Not one little bit. Seeing him made me more afraid, because it made the dreadful fire all the more personal for me. I watched as Mr. McCall pulled on his boots, first one, then the other, he charged down his steps and onto the walk. Mrs. McCall bid him, "Be safe."

He waved at her, and in another quick motion, he stuck his arms into his jacket sleeves and raced toward the fire. My aunt called out to him, "Where is it, Mr. McCall?"

"It's the Murphy house, I was told," Mr. McCall shouted as he turned toward us. With that, he disappeared into the swelling crowd.

I was stunned. "Aunt Mamie, the Murphy house? That's Elizabeth's house! Oh, Aunt Mamie, what's happening?"

"I don't know, Ociee, but grab your cloak and shoes. We'll see for ourselves."

My feet couldn't carry me fast enough. I was throbbing all over. I was both hot and cold at the same time. My friend's house was on fire. What if she was trapped inside? What if she was burning up right that second? "Oh, Aunt Mamie, this is horrible!"

Aunt Mamie stopped short. She gripped me by my shoulders and said, "Now child, calm yourself or we cannot go," she warned. "Do you think you can be very brave for Elizabeth?" She stood for a moment and looked directly into my eyes. I had never seen her as stern.

"Aunt Mamie, I must go," I pleaded, " I'll be brave, you know how brave I can be."

"You keep mindful of that, Ociee dear, you hear me?"

"Yes," I promised.

Our wraps on, she squeezed my trembling hand and toward the Murphys we headed.

Papa had burned rubbish, an old shed once, dead trees and the like. I knew about fire. We were always careful because Papa had cautioned us time and time again. Fact was, fire was the one thing Ben and I never fooled around with. Whenever they were going to burn something, Papa or Fred would dig a big trench around whatever was to be burned. We'd have lots of well water handy. And Ben and I were warned to keep a very safe distance. Until that night, *I thought* I knew about fire. However, there was no way to prepare me for what I was about to see.

Sure enough, it was Elizabeth's house. I'd played there many times. She had a doll bed that matched her own bed. Her papa had built both of them himself. She called her papa, "Father." The doll bed and Elizabeth's bed were walnut, carved out with tiny angels and dogwood blooms. They had high headboards. Hers had a footboard we liked to kick to make the bed rock back and forth. The first time I spent the night, I feared a ghost was going to jump up from behind that high old headboard. Elizabeth laughed and said, "Father wouldn't have dared to built anything with a ghost that could get me." She asked him to come in and tell me that himself. He did. Mr. Murphy came in, kissed Elizabeth goodnight, and hugged me, too. He said, "Elizabeth's bed is ghost-free and so is her doll's bed, Ociee Nash. You two little girls can sleep safe and sound. Angels on your pillow will keep watch. There will be no old ghosts to bother you this night. " I missed my Papa so much that night.

I gripped Aunt Mamie's hand. A big crowd had gathered. My aunt said it looked to her like the whole town had come to help. I didn't much admire that. Fact was, all those people took me right back to the faceless folks squashing me at Mama's funeral. The only thing I cared about was seeing Elizabeth and her folks. I had to see them safe. I searched for them in every face.

"Over here," hollered one big man. Others ran to where he was working. They were pitching things from the Murphy's doors, even from the windows. A huge hole was bashed through the parlor wall. First came Mr. Murphy's desk, then Mrs. Murphy's prized walnut buffet. Its mirror shattered, a door knocked off. Someone carried a chair, one leg missing, its green velvet black with water.

We couldn't see much for the thick stinging smoke. It was making everyone cough. Us, too. I clinched my eyes closed to squeeze wet to clear them.

One man was carried down to the street. A woman wiped his face with wet towels. I was worried he would die. Aunt Mamie said he would not, that he had only to get the smoke from his lungs.

"Elizabeth, Elizabeth, where are you?" I shouted, tears streaming down. "Where are you, Mr. Murphy? And sweet Mrs. Murphy?" Oh, please don't be burned up.

I thought about the little boy who came to our school back home. He had ugly scars on his arms and his neck from a wood stove fire. His skin was lumpy and pink and looked like it hurt him all the time.

"Oh, Elizabeth, you can't look like Percy. Mrs. Murphy, please be all right, and Mr. Murphy, too. I cannot endure another person I love suffering."

I stood in front of Aunt Mamie. She held tight to me with her arms folded across my chest and resting on my shoulders. She leaned over and asked if I was cold. "No, ma'am," I said, "I can't feel anything on my outside for the rumbling going on in my inside."

"There, there," she said, "I believe the Murphys must be out safely by now or we'd have heard. It's just hard to find them in the dark and turmoil."

That was one of those times when my aunt said something mainly out of wishing more than knowing for absolutely sure. But I didn't argue because I was doing the same thing.

I thought about Sunday school. This surely was what Hell was like. It was then we heard a familiar voice. "Mamie, Mamie Nash, is that you?"

"Yes, over here," she shouted.

The voice belonged to Mr. Murphy.

"Frances is over by the tree with Elizabeth, come quickly," he had tears that washed the black soot and stripped his cheeks. He looked at me and rubbed his eyes. "We are, thankfully," he breathed deep, "out of our house." He put his hands to his face and dropped to his knees in front of his family.

I ran and threw my arms around Elizabeth. "Elizabeth, Elizabeth, you're safe!"

She didn't know me. She stood there straight like a soldier with her arms at her side. She was wearing her nightgown, it was pink and wet with water and sticky black dirt. She only looked ahead and didn't as much as blink.

I backed away. Mrs. Murphy shook her head and started to cry. Mr. Murphy reached toward his wife and his little girl. The three of them then huddled together. The night was cold and wet. The fire continued to eat their home.

Quiet. Quiet. Quiet was what they were while everyone else around us shouted. Buckets clanged. Water sloshed. More noise. Fire popped and crackled. Water splashed. The house sizzled and screamed.

People came over to where we were. The Murphys pressed close to each other. Someone brought blankets, another hot tea, another towels, a pillow.

Aunt Mamie took charge. She made sure the three of them got dry and warm, most especially, warm. She had me help. Imagine that, I realized, the Murphy's whole world was burning in a hot, hot fire, yet they could feel nothing but the cold of the night.

I slowly moved next to Elizabeth. She was shaking more than me. Maybe we were shaking each other, I didn't really know. I just sat there next to her. She looked at my eyes and I knew she knew exactly who I was then. I was her best friend again.

That was the first time I understood that people can help someone without saying one single word. My quiet hug was what she needed.

Elizabeth looked up at me and bit her lips together.

"It will be all right," I promised her.

The red glow of sunrise slowly lighted the cold awful night. Aunt Mamie, with her arms around me and Elizabeth, had managed to move us away from all the people. We were cuddled like puppies under a big oak tree nestled close in its strong moss-covered roots. I couldn't tell where the tree left off and Aunt Mamie began. Except for one difference, Aunt Mamie felt good and warm.

Mr. and Mrs. Murphy were talking to the fire fighters. I listened. "Fine work," said Mr. Murphy. "I don't know how you managed to do it. It seems you fellows saved a great deal of our house. We appreciate what you've done."

Mrs. Murphy, eyes shut, said through her tears, "We are deeply grateful. Our family is safe and little else matters." She rested her head on her husband's shoulder.

My aunt hugged us two girls tightly and said, "Look, Elizabeth, Ociee, the good Lord is sending us His morning sun. Everything is going to seem better in the light of day."

Minutes later, Mr. Murphy walked over to Elizabeth. "Look what one of the volunteers found, darling. Not a scratch on it that I can't repair for you."

He handed Elizabeth the doll's bed.

"Oh, Father!" she said taking the bed and putting it on the ground beside the oak tree. Elizabeth looked down smiling at her rescued treasure.

With that, Mrs. Murphy came toward us. She was carrying Elizabeth's baby doll. It had black dirt smudged on its face and hands and its dress was soaked clean through. Using a fresh soapy towel someone handed to her, Mrs. Murphy was trying to clean the doll. She gave it to Elizabeth, who placed her gently on the bed.

I kneeled down and placed my fingertips on the doll.

"Angels on your pillow keep watch," I said.

"Yes, indeed, those angels were busy with us tonight," said Mrs. Murphy.

I was so glad that I hadn't lost another mama.

20

Just after the sun rose, the fire had almost finishing burning out. Many of the volunteer firemen began to leave for their own homes. The men milled past the Murphys offering their sympathies for the misfortune. Women promised food and clothes. Everyone wanted to help clean and fix what remained of the house and what was saved from inside.

Aunt Mamie said I could invite Elizabeth and her folks to rest at our house. Mr. Murphy smiled as best he could and said, "I'll say 'yes' for Frances and Elizabeth. Thank you. But I feel that I must stay right here as long as any of these courageous people remain."

Mrs. Murphy started to argue with her husband, saying how tired he looked. Mr. Murphy couldn't as much as listen. Aunt Mamie said that he was intent on kicking through the rubble and trying to make sense of the night's damage. I knew that was how my Papa would have been acting if it'd been our house. Sometimes papas have to think of what they have to do and not think much on how exhausted they must be. Papa was like that, I knew.

Upstairs at Aunt Mamie's, Mrs. Murphy and Elizabeth got bathed. On the guest room bed I laid out two fresh ironed cotton gowns for them to wear. Mrs. Murphy pulled her towel dried hair back from her face and rubbed Elizabeth's wet hair with another towel. I saw them hug one another really tight. I turned away from the door.

We wanted to fix scrambled eggs and bacon, but all either of them felt up to was some soup. Mrs. Murphy was trembling so that I took the spoon from her hand and offered to feed her myself.

"Thank you, dear," she said. "Gracious, don't I look silly, like a little baby?"

"No ma'am, you don't look silly, not at all. You can't steady yourself to eat because you're so awful upset. You should have seen me and my brothers the morning I was leaving for Asheville. Papa had fixed the biggest breakfast you ever saw and not one of us swallowed a single bite. Sometimes a body won't work like we want it to. Here, let me do this for you, please let me."

Mrs. Murphy nodded.

"Mmm," she said closing her lips. "Thank you, Ociee, this is quite tasty."

I looked at Elizabeth, who was watching. "Do you want to do this for your mama instead of me?"

"No, I couldn't," she showed me how her own hands were shaking.

Aunt Mamie said, "Let's have that spoon, child, I can't be left out." She dipped a spoon in Elizabeth's soup bowl. "Ociee, let's see which of these girls can eat the most chicken soup."

I decided to play a joke on my friend. She wasn't much of a cat person. I asked my aunt, "Is that spoon you're using for Elizabeth the one you just used to give Miss Kitty Cat a taste of cream? Thought I saw Miss Kitty Cat lick right from that very spoon, lick, lick, scratchy, itchy kitty cat tongue lick."

"What!" squealed Elizabeth, making a terrible wrinkled-nose face.

"Ociee Nash, of course not!" scowled Aunt Mamie. "What in the world's gotten into you?" Then she saw me wink.

"Oh yes, on second thought, this is the kitty's spoon," she said looking at it very carefully.

Elizabeth was gulping down the closest glass of water.

Aunt Mamie played into my game saying, "Or was this the spoon that I used to dig up that fat wiggly fishing worm from the window box? Ociee, I do believe I used this spoon for *both* tasks. Here, Elizabeth, do have another delicious taste of our soup."

Elizabeth sat, eyes wide, lips clinched.

Mrs. Murphy started to snicker.

Before another second went by, Elizabeth realized she had been the victim of some of our teasing. The fire was forgotten, if only for a moment. The four of us sat at the kitchen table, laughing hysterically. Both Elizabeth and Mrs. Murphy ate all their soup and asked for seconds.

When it seemed they had their fill, Aunt Mamie suggested, "It's off to bed with the both of you and Ociee and myself, as well. It has been a long, long night, I think it's best that we all try to get some rest."

"Yes, I am suddenly very tired," said Mrs. Murphy. She reached for Elizabeth's hand. "Do you want to lie down with me, dear?"

"Oh, or with me?" I asked my friend. Aunt Mamie nodded her approval.

"Well, I'd like to choose Ociee," she said. "If, Mother, you don't mind."

"That's fine, I think I can do without your wiggles."

Mrs. Murphy was the first to speak as we climbed the stairs. "I cannot thank you Nashes enough."

Aunt Mamie answered, "You are truly welcome."

I answered, too, "Very, very welcome."

You Nashes, that was strange to hear. I had always thought of Nash as my name, and as Papa's, Mama's, and as my brothers'. I also knew full well that Aunt Mamie was Mamie Nash. Even so, hearing "You Nashes" struck me as odd. That was simply one of those things I never thought about until it was said out loud.

You Nashes, how nice that felt to my ears.

Elizabeth kissed her mother goodnight, and I kissed my aunt. The women tucked the two of us girls into my bed and covered us with Mama's quilt. Toasty warm and safe like a cocoon, that quilt had always provided me with shelter. That unsteady morning after the Murphy's fire, I hoped it offered the same kind comfort to my friend.

"Cat tongues, for heaven's sake," fussed Elizabeth.

112

"Wiggly worms," I answered.

"Cat tongues and wiggley worms!" We laughed. We laughed and laughed uncontrollably. Then, without another word, we both started to cry. We hugged tightly and cried all the more.

Finally, there were no more tears.

"Elizabeth, angels on your pillow," I said as we closed our eyes.

"Yours, too," she said.

We slept.

I had what seemed a good rest. Sometime, in the late morning, I thought I'd counted ten chimes on the hall clock, there came a knock at the front door. I jumped up and raced down the stairs to keep the others from being waked up. At the door stood Mrs. McCall, our neighbor from next door.

I put my finger to my lips, "Shhh. I'm the only one awake just yet. Mrs. Murphy and Elizabeth are here sleeping. And Aunt Mamie's probably still asleep, too. "

"Oh my. Of course, I'll come back later," she said as she started to turn away.

"Well, actually, please come in. Come back to the kitchen, if you will," I asked.

I was wanting to know if anything else had happened while we slept. Mrs. McCall would know. While she talked, I fixed her a cup of tea and washed up the chicken soup dishes. I asked if Mr. McCall had withstood the fire fighting during the awful night.

She said indeed, he had arrived home only an hour ago and was dragging. She said she had him clean up and climb right into bed. "Poor man, he was whipped," she explained. Mrs. McCall said the only thing her husband told her was they had saved a good bit of the house, more than they had expected to at the fire's beginning.

"You best tell them that good news when they first wake up," she suggested. "Although I would imagine that Mr. Murphy will be by here in not too much longer. He'll be wanting to share that news with his family." Mrs. McCall said the whole community would be pitching in to help the Murphys. She said, "The first thing we'll do will be the washing and cleaning to save the household items." She also said there would be contributions from neighbors, dishes and the sort. "A time of crisis is when you really get the flavor of the folks who care," said Mrs. McCall. "I know that for a fact, because we once had a fire. Along with our tragedy we discovered the enormous kindness of our own good neighbors."

"Gracious, you did?" I asked, almost afraid to hear, but curious all the same.

"Yes, we did. Not in our house now, but in one south of here. Not to worry, it was a very small crisis compared to the Murphys'. It was just enough that Mr. McCall himself was encouraged to join the fire department. Been a fire fighter ever since, felt he owed it to the citizens of Asheville."

I was beginning to think everybody in the world had bad things happen to them. It surely seemed that way to me. But, like the McCalls, I was seeing how people often let hard times teach them to do neighborly things for folks. Surely sounded right to me.

"I'm going to join the fire department!" I announced.

"Goodness, child, you are just a little thing! You can't be doing such a task," she laughed.

That made me mad. "I may be little, but I'm very brave," I said rather rudely. "Whoops, I'm sorry, Mrs. McCall. It's pretty normal for me to let my eagerness jump way ahead of details."

She just sat there looking at me with her mouth open. I never knew what folks were thinking, so I took her quiet as a sign of interest. That was the main reason I kept on talking, "Besides being brave, I'm strong and smart, too!"

Then, I had to catch myself. I understood I should stop ranting and apologize for what my aunt may have called my "frontier spirit."

"Please excuse me for carrying on so," I said. " It could be because I grew up out West."

"Not at all, Ociee," said Mrs. McCall. She was almost laughing again, not making fun, but in a nice way. "I think your spirit is just the kind of enthusiasm we must have to help the Murphys." She continued, "I originally came over to get your aunt's assistance, but it looks like I have the perfect Nash to do the job we have ahead. You and I can make a list of what needs to be done. Let's allow Mamie to get her rest."

"Yes, ma'am," I said. My nose poked up in the air. Proud as a peacock was what I was.

21

Mrs. McCall was right about how much the people in town wanted to help. Our back porch and our basement were soon chucked full of furniture, clothes, kitchen supplies, linens, most anything a family would need.

My job was to write in a special book a list of the kindnesses that folks performed. Mrs. Murphy said she planned to look back through my book once she moved back into her own home. She said she was going to write thank you letters to every person in it. Knowing that made me all the more careful with my note taking.

Every day, more neighbors came to drop off the Murphys' own items which they had taken home to clean, to wash, or to rescue in some way. I well remembered the saddest day since the fire. Mrs. Murphy was told that all of her treasured quilts were ruined. Aunt Mamie suggested one last attempt to get rid of the terrible smell of smoke. I helped.

Early the next morning, we carried her three favorites outside to hang on our clothesline. We checked once an hour. My aunt said, "It is the most perfect day. The Lord has blessed us with a soft and gentle breeze and beautiful bright sunshine."

Even God's sun couldn't suck out the fire's cruel stink. Late that afternoon, Mrs. Murphy sat and cried.

I went upstairs. Her sadness followed me up into my room. "Mama," I said, as I looked deeply into her eyes in my tiny painting, "I think you would approve of me for doing this." I went down the steps carrying Mama's quilt.

Holding it out to Elizabeth's mother, I said, "Mrs. Murphy, here is a new quilt to replace one that the fire took away."

"Oh, dear child, how lovely. I am truly overwhelmed;" wiping her eyes, she swooned.

There wasn't another sound in the room.

Mrs. Murphy unfolded Mama's quilt out across my aunt's daybed. "Who crafted such a fine piece? Your Aunt Mamie, I would guess. Just look at the beauty of her work."

Aunt Mamie shook her head 'no.'

I was so proud. I said, "It was Mama's, my Mama's very fine work."

Elizabeth had come in and stood with her mother. She said, "Ociee brought it here all the way from Mississippi. Her mother sewed it on their farm, *way out West,* just imagine!"

"Come over here, Ociee, dear," said Mrs. Murphy. "Tell me more, if you please."

I started explaining about pieces from Fred's dress, from Papa's shirts, and my school dresses, a doll coat, baby's clothes, Aunt Mamie's and Mama's. Mrs. Murphy listened. I told her how Mama and Aunt Mamie even swapped pieces of material between Abbeville and Mississippi through the U.S. mail. My aunt laughed about that and added her own details of our family's shared stories.

I talked of Mama's quilting bees and how Papa teased her about having 'chatting bees' instead. Mrs. Murphy laughed about that and said she wished she had known Mama. "I think we would have been great friends, friends just like you and my Elizabeth."

I smiled.

Mrs. Murphy put her arm around me and said, "Ociee, you cannot know how much this gift touches me. You are offering me a piece of yourself, of your very own history. I have so enjoyed hearing your quilt's stories. I have relished watching you tell them," she added.

I lowered my head. I was feeling a tad embarrassed at the way she went on so. But, at the same time, I was fairly pleased with myself. I touched Mama's locket. It was the one piece of Mama I could never part with.

Mrs. Murphy then said, "As moved as I am, I must insist you keep this beautiful creation for yourself. Ociee, I am sincerely

117

grateful that you want me to have it, but a lovely work of art like this is a priceless heirloom for your own family." She determined, "The truth is that the quilt will become even more precious to you now, because you have been willing to share it with us."

"I don't understand," I said.

"You will, dear, you will. Just promise you will always keep your dear heart as generous as it is this day."

"Yes ma'am, I guess you know best, being that you are a mama yourself."

Mrs. Murphy hugged me extra close. It felt like Aunt Mamie's hugs except there wasn't quite as much of Mrs. Murphy to hug back.

Aunt Mamie was crying.

"Gracious sakes, first, Mrs. Murphy was sad, so I tried to cheer her up. And that made you sad, Aunt Mamie," I said. "You grown people are hard for me to understand sometimes."

Aunt Mamie explained, "Sometimes us grown people cry when they are very proud of their nieces. At least that is certainly why this aunt is crying. Rest assured, your Mama is most definitely fluttering her angel's wings for her daughter this afternoon."

I figured, all in all, I had done the best I could.

The Murphys' house was being built back. We'd go see it everyday on the way home from school. In the meantime, Elizabeth and her parents stayed with us. It was grand, almost like having a sister or maybe better. We did everything together and us two girls even liked sharing the chores. Of course, Elizabeth wasn't skilled enough to help with the seamstress duties. Aunt Mamie explained that took months of practice along with our "family talent." I had to grin.

118

When it appeared that the house was going to take longer than expected, the Murphys decided to share some time with relatives in North Georgia. I fought that. I wanted to keep Elizabeth forever, but Aunt Mamie said her folks would miss her too much. She reminded me of how much Ben and Papa and Fred were missing their Ociee. "The Murphys simply couldn't do without her," she said to me. All I could think was my own selfish thoughts of missing her, but I was also thinking of my *generous heart.*

The night before they left for Georgia, we planned to celebrate my birthday. But it didn't start out anything like a party. There I was, turning ten years old in just two days and I wasn't the least bit happy, nor was Elizabeth, for that matter. At first, I thought she was jealous because I was turning ten and she would be stuck at nine until January 31. I asked and she said 'no.' Just no.

We hardly ate any of Aunt Mamie's cake, chocolate even, because we were too grumpy about being separated the day after the next. Guess I misplaced *my generous heart* for the evening. For my wish, I wished the Murphys wouldn't go at all, or that the house would magically be finished by morning, or that the fire never happened in the first place.

I must have been thinking too much about that fire when my aunt lighted the candles. Not meaning to at all, I spit on those ten birthday candles.

Aunt Mamie said, "You just added extra sugar, Ociee. It needed more any way."

Everybody laughed.

Part of my wish came true. Mrs. Murphy pledged, crossed her heart and all, that she would bring Elizabeth and herself home as soon as she could. So, at very least, they weren't going to be gone forever.

I did also get them to promise they'd be extra friendly to everyone who was traveling on the train, especially to all the children. I told them, "You meet lots of interesting people that way. Mind you, you may meet some snooty people, but just ignore them. Consider that *their* loss."

Elizabeth paid careful attention to me, because she liked to hear my traveling stories. Elizabeth didn't have my travel experience. Also she tended to believe every word I said, even if I exaggerated. I wanted her to picture how calm I was *early* on my own train trip. Truthfully, I had been very afraid. But that would always remain my secret.

"Ociee, I have a big favor to ask you ," said Elizabeth. "Will you take care of my doll bed for me while we're gone? Please? Mother says it'd be too hard to take with us on the train. You're the only person I trust completely with it, especially since Father has worked so hard to get the smoke smell out."

"Yes, I'll be glad to," I said. I really loved the idea of having a little part of my very best friend with me while she was gone. Gone! "Elizabeth, what will I do without you?"

We managed to have fun on that, our very last night. I went on to school the next morning pretending nothing was different. But it was. Just after breakfast, I hugged the Murphys good-bye. It hurt near about as much as when I left home.

Two days later, my real actual birthday came. I couldn't be cheered up. Aunt Mamie came up with another one of her plans. "We will celebrate your birthday, one month to the day late. So, Ociee Nash, this year, your birthday is officially December 8. How's that?"

I was so crabby that I just said, "It's all right." Aunt Mamie knew me well enough by then to know that was what I said when I was sad. But she also knew that I would have to take a certain amount of time to get used to Elizabeth's being gone.

In the weeks that passed, there was one good thing that happened. Going to the Post Office was even more exciting because Elizabeth was a better letter writer than Papa, Fred and Ben all put together. We had already written to each other four times. In her first letter, Elizabeth said she had fun on the train, but she upchucked twice. She upchucked on her doll. That poor baby doll, first a fire, then a sick mama. I probably should have taken care of her doll for her, but she would never have agreed to that. Especially after almost losing her to the fire.

Mr. Murphy was living in Mrs. Lilly's boarding house, the same one where Mr. Lynch, the buggy driver, lived. We had Mr. Murphy over for dinner at least one or two nights every week.

One of the nights that Mr. Murphy was coming, I asked Aunt Mamie, if Mr. Lynch might come along, too. I told her that I thought he'd like the change. "He must get awfully tired of Mrs. Lilly's food, because he eats at the church any chance he gets." That was a little more than Mr. Lynch said, but I wanted my aunt to say it was fine with her.

"Oh my, we had talked about fixing him a basket, hadn't we? Here, I up and forgot all about doing so."

She agreed. I knew she would.

It wasn't hard to find Mr. Lynch. It was a Saturday, and he was to spend most of the afternoon in his buggy carrying fares around our neighborhood. I saw him and ran out once when he was driving an empty buggy. "Hello, Old Horse, hello, Mr. Lynch. Guess what, Aunt Mamie says you can come to dinner this very night!"

Just like Aunt Mamie, he said 'yes,' too.

I knew he would.

22

At six o'clock sharp, up the street came Mr. Lynch. He was walking with Mr. Murphy. I don't suppose I'd ever seen Mr. Lynch walk more than a few feet. He was always sitting and driving his buggy.

"Where's Old Horse?" I shouted as I ran to greet our company.

Mr. Lynch said, "Was I supposed to bring him? Just how were you going to sit him at your table, Ociee?"

Mr. Murphy laughed, and I did, too.

"I'm afraid my horse isn't much good at visiting in the evenings. He has to catch up on his rest, don't you know. It's the only time he's not working, you understand."

I guessed I'd never thought about that. Inside we went.

"Something smells mighty good, Mamie," said Mr. Murphy.

My aunt came from the kitchen wiping her hands on her apron.

"Ociee helped me to prepare our meal, it's fried chicken and rice, pole beans, and biscuits. I suspect it's the chicken that's got your attention." She turned her attention to Mr. Lynch, "We're delighted you both could join us."

Mr. Murphy grinned and Mr. Lynch said, "Thank you , Miss Nash."

We walked into the parlor. I was feeling very grown up, like a real lady.

"Mr. Lynch, we fixed three different pies for you to choose from. We have apple, blueberry, and lemon meringue."

Mr. Lynch replied, "Can I choose, let me see, how about some of all three?"

"Why, of course, you can," said Aunt Mamie, "I can see why my little niece has selected you to be her friend. Seems that you two think alike."

Dinner time was special at 66 Charlotte Street. In those days, most children weren't allowed to eat with grown people, but Aunt Mamie didn't feel that way about our meals. She was like Papa about that. My aunt enjoyed the company of children. She and I often took our meals in the dining room. I'd set the table with lovely cloths and flowers. And, we always ate in the dining room if we had a guest.

That night before we sat down, Mr. Murphy told us he had a letter to read from his family in Georgia. Elizabeth! Mr. Lynch said he would enjoy hearing it, too. He told us he was interested in everyone from his hometown. Mr. Lynch was polite, I liked that about him.

In the letter, Mrs. Murphy said she and Elizabeth were missing us all, even though they appreciated where they were. "Up in the mountains it's apple season," she wrote. "Elizabeth has picked enough apples for all of Asheville. We'll bring as many as we can when we come home."

"When we come home," I thought, I just wished that everybody who liked everybody else could live close by one another. For once, I was too busy missing someone else to be thinking of missing Mississippi.

That night at supper, Mr. Lynch and my aunt laughed and talked. First they talked to Mr. Murphy, then to me, then back to Mr. Murphy. They talked about Asheville and how fast the town was growing. When I was chatting with Mr. Murphy, I noticed that my Aunt Mamie and Mr. Lynch were talking to each other.

For dessert, Mr. Lynch did actually eat three whole pieces of pie. He reared back in his chair and said, "Better than any I've eaten at the church, Miss Nash."

"I got you there, Mr. Lynch, I've taken many pies to the church, and you've eaten them before. I watch who eats my baking. I believe you're just flattering me because you're here in our home tonight," she teased.

"Not at all, not at all," he argued. "Maybe things just taste better when they're eaten in the home where they've been baked." Then he added, "Call me George, if you don't mind. I hope you don't think me too forward."

I didn't let her say a word. "George! George is my Papa's name!"

Mr. Murphy sat there chuckling.

I didn't think anything was so funny. I just felt real happy. And that was a mighty good feeling.

The end of November, Papa, Ben and Fred experienced their first Thanksgiving without their Ociee. First no Mama, and then no me. Neighbors invited Papa and the boys over, he wrote to say. But he didn't seem one bit cheerful about it. He tried to joke writing he planned to bring home the turkey carcass just to have the smell of leftovers in the air at home. Papa could make jokes, and he did much of the time. That was how he acted so he didn't have to let on to people how bad he was grieving.

Aunt Mamie's house did smell exactly like home was supposed to smell. When Thursday finally arrived, we had spent days cooking our dressing, sweet potatoes, special cranberry relish, the turkey. That was such fun that I nearly forgot about being homesick. Well, almost nearly, anyway.

We stuffed our turkey until Aunt Mamie said it looked just like her. "Put my apron around the bird," she suggested. "Your Mr. Lynch won't guess which one of us is the turkey."

Mr. Lynch arrived at 1 o'clock on Thanksgiving Day. It was clear he knew which was which, because he gave my aunt a kiss. I snickered.

After our meal, Mr. Lynch said, "Absolutely delicious, ladies. Now I'll plan to help you with all these dishes in a bit. But first, let's sit on the porch for a spell and enjoy the warm sun. Days are getting shorter, and we won't have this opportunity come winter."

It was a good day. In fact, I wrote that very sentence in my book. I'd taken to writing down things. That way, I could remember more. I wished I'd done that in Mississippi.

The longer I was in Asheville, the more I was forgetting where things were at home. Not little things. I knew where we kept Mama's hat, or Papa's record books, or Ben's baby rattle. I was having trouble placing where the big things were. Where was the oak out in the pasture. Middle? Closer to the barn? Or just how did we go to Miss May's house? What type of store was next door to the telegraph office in Abbeville? I believed it was dry goods, but my mind's eye was fast fading.

On the morning of December 8, Aunt Mamie burst into my room at 6 A.M. "Happy birthday, happy birthday, happy birthday to you!"

I remembered we were to celebrate a month later because of Elizabeth's leaving. What fun that was to be. "Yes, Aunt Mamie, Happy Birthday to me, today!"

She had gotten up extra early and even canceled her customers's appointments for the whole day. We sat down to breakfast. My aunt had fixed my very favorite. We had pancakes with powdered sugar, sausage, and hot chocolate.

We almost had birthday cake and icing, but we decided to hold back. "I want to have something left for later," I said.

"My goodness, young lady, aren't you the grown woman, imagine, just ten years and one month old *today* and you have already learned the art of how to save and savor," she said.

"Save and savor" was to become something we shared. We saved and savored for decades to come.

After breakfast, we sipped our drinks, her coffee with cream, my chocolate, also with cream. We drank from our favorite teacups. And we sat for an hour and a half. I'd gotten to where I could sit for hours without as much as a wiggle, at least when talking to Aunt Mamie. That didn't work as well in school, however. Aunt Mamie continued to be much more interesting than school.

During the day of my tenth year plus one month, we went for a walk, we had ice cream and cake and discussed many things. My favorite subject was Mama. I loved to hear about Mama as a young lady, long years before she was mine. About her being courted by Papa. It made me laugh out loud when Aunt Mamie told me how Papa rehearsed carefully every word he was going to say to her during their evenings out.

"Your Papa had two left feet," she told. "Lord knows, I tried to teach him to dance. We practiced and practiced. I often wondered if Bertie's toes were as bruised as mine."

"Bertie." That was another strange thing, to hear Mama's real name. Bertie was shortened from Alberta. I'd heard it before, more when Mama was alive. Papa almost always called her "your Mama," after she died.

"Aunt Mamie," I asked, "did you ever hear Papa's silly verses he wrote to make Mama laugh?"

"Can you say one to me, dear?" she asked.

I remembered my favorite:

> *Some folks may think*
> *I'm just being partial,*
> *When I tell them my Bertie's*
> *The prettiest girl in Marshall.*

Aunt Mamie looked at me. I looked at her and we got so tickled. Fact was, we laughed until tears came. Aunt Mamie took off her glasses and wiped her eyes saying, "Gracious, goodness sakes alive, George's poetry is no better than his dancing!"

I pretended to be mad. "Well, I like it." But I couldn't hold back and I started laughing again.

"Ociee, I'm certain your Mama liked it, too, and your Papa's dancing as well. That's what was so dear about her. She did love my brother."

"And he still loves Mama," I added.

"Ociee, sweet darling, I meant to give you this first thing this morning. It's a letter from that very Papa of yours. Enjoy it while I wash up these dishes. There will be no work for you this day."

I opened my letter.

Papa wrote to say "Happy Birthday," again.

Dearest Ociee,

Little wonder you are happy in Asheville. I don't know another little girl who has <u>two</u> birthdays in one year. I'll not send a second gift, for Ben would be eaten up with being jealous. I will write to tell you again that I love you dearly.

And I miss you so much my heart hurts anytime I look where you are supposed to be. We all miss you. We miss you on the porch, or out in the chicken yard, or at the kitchen table.

Any spot you picture at home is empty with you absent from it. I'm making you sad, Miss Birthday Girl. Forgive your old Papa. I just love you that's all.

I'll write about Ben. He was giving <u>fits</u> to his new teacher. God bless her. The nice lady is named Miss Brown. One day (or one of the days) he had to stay after school to practice his spelling, Miss Brown stayed to talk with him. Said she also lost her mama when she was young. She's a kind lady, smart, and she gives Ben a little longer lead and a lot more time than the other children.

Ben says to say, "Happy Birthday, double digits." He says to tell you he can count his years on his fingers – and one <u>toe</u>! And he wants you to tell him the very first time you get to play in snow. I told that boy to write you himself – said he would.

The big news here is twofold. First of all, your brother Fred is courting Rebecca pretty seriously. Tell your Aunt Mamie, Fred's foolishness reminds me of a certain brother of hers, twenty or so years ago. I'll tell you, can you keep a secret? From the looks of things, we might be having a wedding down the road.

"Aunt Mamie," I screamed out and ran back to the kitchen, "Fred's getting married!" Then, I remembered the keeping a secret part of Papa's letter. Oh dear. "Aunt Mamie, please forget I said that."

"Ociee, dearest, that's a hard thing to forget," she said. "I'll try, but goodness, I may burst wide open over a wedding! When, dear, is there a date set?"

I read again, *"down the road"* is all Papa said about that. I put the letter aside and told my aunt about Fred's girl. I tried to make Rebecca sound better than the silly old town girl she truly was. Aunt Mamie was drying up the dishes. "Ociee, don't be so hard on her. I, myself, am a 'town girl.' You seem to like me well enough."

"You're different!"

"Ociee." Aunt Mamie gave me one of her looks.

"Yes ma'am. But I know *you* can tell the difference between a horse and a cornstalk. Rebecca can't."

"Ociee Nash, she couldn't be that bad! Besides, she can learn. The girl is likely so taken with your brother, she isn't looking at cornstalks or horses long enough to see the difference," said my aunt. "Your Papa has mentioned a special girl for Fred to me as well. And he seems pleased with the young lady."

"Well, maybe. I'll be reading the rest of Papa's letter now."

Rebecca Nash, Rebecca Nash, I guessed I might as well get used the way that sounded. "Down the road" or not, she was one lucky girl to have Fred courting her, I decided.

We're about done with the pre-winter chores. Always something else to do on this old farm. I suppose my lack of enthusiasm is showing itself to you. I know you are working hard, too, in school. Your grades are excellent. Surely am proud of my girl. I know your Mama's proud of you, too.

Have a Happy Birthday, eat some cake for me and your brothers. Always know that three men folk in Mississippi miss our Ociee girl so very much.

Love,

Your Papa.

What was it about letters? I'd get one and want another. I'd read one and want more words. I loved Aunt Mamie. But I wanted my Papa and my farm and I wanted my Ben and my Fred.

Dear me, that news about Fred's Rebecca. Rebecca, Rebecca Nash. I figured it was none of my business. Come to think of it, I might just sit down and write Fred. No, best not. Papa asked me not to blab and I'd already done it.

Fred picked her out. I guessed she'd have to do. Papa seemed to be happy enough that he told me about it. I wondered if Ben knew.

And Aunt Mamie, well, she grew up in a town, so maybe somewhere hidden inside Rebecca was a grown lady who would turn out to be smart and interesting like Aunt Mamie.

Ociee Nash, you just as well might get yourself used to one more change. At least the one around that corner wasn't a sad thing, like your best friend leaving, or a dreadful fire, or Mama dying.

23

Being ten was not at all what I thought it would be. I was still short. And I couldn't tell that I was one tad smarter. Aunt Mamie reasoned, "That's because you got extra smart while you were nine and you're still catching up with yourself."

That made sense to me.

Thanksgiving had been a happy surprise, so I figured the same thing would happen for us on Christmas. I was especially looking forward to Elizabeth coming back from Georgia. The bad news came six days before Christmas Eve.

> *Dear Ociee,*
>
> *We waited until the last possible minute to decide. I didn't decide at all. I just wanted to come home to my house on my street and see my best friend. Mother and Father are sad as they can be. Our house won't be ready in time for us to be home Christmas. I said we could put our tree in our empty house right in the middle of all those slow as molasses workers. Mother said that wouldn't do. That we must hold on to the truth that our next Christmas will be all the better because of these bad times. Thank goodness, Father is coming to Georgia to join us.*
>
> *I hope you will have fun with your dear Aunt Mamie. Be sure and put holly on <u>our</u> doll's bed, as that is a tradition. At least, Ociee, that gives us something to share.*
>
> *Mother says you and I can have Christmas as soon as we come home. She said you and I, your Aunt Mamie, and she will have a jolly old time then even if it's Valentine's Day.*
>
> *With love, your very best, too sad, and far away true friend,*
> *Elizabeth*

Valentine's Day? My big toe! I decided right then and there to go by the Murphys' house each and every day on my way home from school and make certain those men were working on that house. I would see to it.

Aunt Mamie was determined to make Christmas especially festive for me. We took Mr. Lynch to church, and afterwards, back to our house for dinner. He brought a present for each of us! They were hidden in the buggy. He gave Aunt Mamie a beautiful white lace handkerchief which came all the way from Paris, France. He told me he drove Old Horse across the Atlantic Ocean to pick the perfect one for her. I knew he was making that up, but I liked that he said it.

I loved my Christmas present from Mr. Lynch. It was wrapped in red paper with a green bow. I shook it, and he warned me, "Careful, Ociee, it may break." I carefully took off the box's top and there, wrapped in tissue, was a china figurine.

"It's Old Horse!" I cheered.

"My gracious, the very horse who carried you home to me," said my aunt. "Why, he's perfect. You'd think he posed for it."

"I'm glad you like the gift, too, but don't you be forgetting who drove that buggy," he reminded her.

"Why I'm not about to forget, George. In fact, we girls have a Christmas remembrance for that dear driver," said my aunt. She handed him our present. I could have popped for twittering. Not able to stand it another second, I jumped up and stood right over him.

Mr. Lynch was excited, too. He tore off the wrapping and found our surprise. Aunt Mamie and I had worked for hours every evening after our customers' sewing was complete. We knitted him a warm woolen sweater. It was deep red and fastened with fine ivory buttons.

"Oh my, I've never seen anything so beautiful," he uttered.

"All the parts that are *redone* are my knitting," I explained, "It had to be perfect before we would give to you."

131

Mr. Lynch said, "That 'redoing' will likely serve to make it a stronger weave."

"Really?!" I asked.

"I'm sure that's right if George Lynch says so," assured Aunt Mamie.

He smiled.

"That's why we had to send you home from supper so early these last few weeks," I admitted to him. "We were running short on time, and we didn't want to give away our secret."

He winked, "I never suspected a thing."

"George Lynch, I've watched you drive up and down this street for years, and you always looked as though you were freezing to death from November all the way until the dogwoods bloomed. I told Ociee, and we made up our minds to do something about that," said my aunt.

He smiled real big. "I'm glad you did."

To try out the new sweater, I suggested that we go for a buggy ride. We did, Mr. Lynch rode us all over the whole entire town of Asheville.

"Are you showing off your Christmas sweater, Mr. Lynch?" I asked.

"Why, I'm showing off my sweater and the both of you charming ladies," he said holding his head high.

"Ociee, I must thank you. I've been passing your aunt's house for all these years. Yes, I waved a bit, admired the lovely lady on the front porch, but if you hadn't come here, I would have missed the *two* of you."

"George Lynch, you rascal," said my aunt.

It was cold, just exactly as cold as we wanted it to be. We snuggled together all squished in the front seat. Old Horse acted as proud as he if he was carrying the Vanderbilts.

Mr. Lynch told us Old Horse preferred the cold weather. "The coolness encourages him to move faster," he explained. "And Ociee, you gave him that taste of sugar. You insist that gives him energy, too. So we better hang on tight!"

"Merry Christmas, fast Old Horse!"

"Merry Christmas!" I shouted to people I knew.
"Merry Christmas!" I shouted to people I didn't know.
"Merry, Merry Christmas!" I shouted into the cool winter air.

Days before, I had decided I would pretend as if I was having a happy time just so Aunt Mamie would know I was grateful to her for being so kind to me. I'd pretend to please Papa for that was the way he expected me to behave. I wanted to be as happy acting as I could also because Mama would want that.

The fact was I wasn't play-acting at all. It was true. There I was, riding in the buggy with Aunt Mamie and Mr. Lynch. I was waving to every person on the streets of Asheville.

It was cold. New snow was falling. I'd write to Ben. Snow was the only thing he cared about in the whole state of North Carolina, well, snow and the mountains, and me, of course.

Out of the clear winter sky, a sudden pang of homesickness hit just a like a splash of cold water. It was Christmas, and I missed my Ben. I did miss Fred, and Papa, too. I missed my family something awful.

I closed my eyes and thought of home. I thought of our Christmas oranges and candies that always filled our stockings. I had a new stocking in Asheville. It was filled too, but with different things. I hoped Papa and my brothers liked their presents.

Aunt Mamie had helped me to make them each a new shirt. Fred's was brown. I chose a quiet color for him, because he didn't so much like to be noticed. Ben's was bright red as he was just the opposite of Fred. Papa's was blue plaid and the hardest to make. The plaid had to match everywhere it joined. I left one tooth mark in the collar—my signature.

We sent the presents in one big box on the train weeks ago. Papa wrote that it got there safely. He also said he was having the hardest time keeping Ben from opening it. It mattered that I sent presents to everyone. I wasn't there, and they needed something in my place.

"Merry, Merry Christmas," I whispered with no sound, wishing Papa could hear me say it.

"Ociee, you're mighty quiet," said Aunt Mamie. "Are you frozen solid, dear? Hurry home, George."

"I'm fine, truly, Aunt Mamie. Just hungry, that's all."

"See, George, let's get this cold hungry child back home," she said.

Christmas dinner was Thanksgiving dinner and more. Right smack dab in the middle of carving the turkey, Mr. Lynch put down the knife and fork and asked, "Mamie Nash, will you and Ociee marry me?"

24

"George Lynch, have you gone daft?" said my aunt as she fanned herself with the table napkin.

"Indeed, I am as sane as a man can be," he replied.

I sat there dumb as a post.

"Mr. Lynch, I am a maiden lady," she argued.

"I like to think you were waiting for me," he beamed.

"Why, I have responsibilities, George, my seamstress shop, my precious darling Ociee."

"I considered your Ociee, Mamie, that was the reason I proposed to the both of you. Ociee is a very special part of your life," he said looking at me. "Until she goes home to her Papa, I'll look after her, with you."

I smiled with my lips locked tight together.

"As for your seamstressing, I surely will continue on as a buggy driver," he insisted. "I wouldn't ask you to change anything about yourself, Mamie. Except if you will, to become Mrs. Lynch."

My aunt looked suddenly very sad, "George, I am sorry to say, but I could consider no such thing."

I stayed quiet. That was truly grown folks territory. I looked at Mr. Lynch who was shifting his food around, not taking a taste of anything. Aunt Mamie was completely different. She was taking strange fast bites, mixing things together, eating entirely too fast. Her fork was klinking all over her china plate. Goodness, my aunt's teeth were clicking like the needle on her sewing machine. Tick, tick, tick, tick.

I popped. "I am so sorry, Aunt Mamie. I know this is rude and not at all ladylike, but I must interrupt all this awful quiet."

"Ociee, best watch yourself," she insisted. Her eyebrow raised so I knew I was overstepping her rules.

Swallowing hard, I went on, "I am, I am watching myself be really, really uneasy here. I am uneasy, and it's Christmas, and that makes sad things all the worse."

"Oh, dear Ociee," said my aunt.

I had jumped into the pond and had to swim.

"When I came to Asheville, now almost five months ago, I didn't know anybody, 'cept my Aunt Mamie and not as half as well as I do now. Here we are, 'course, I'm ten." I saw Mr. Lynch chortle. "Anyway, I will be going home one of these days and you will both be lonely. I know how difficult that can be. I wish you would think on Mr. Lynch's proposal, Aunt Mamie. Will you please? I just can't bear to think of more lonely folks for me to worry about. "

"Well? Aunt Mamie," said Mr. Lynch.

"Well? Mr. Lynch," said Aunt Mamie.

Then was the time for me to lock my lips tight again.

"Eat your dinner, George, I will think about your proposal."

"You will?" he shouted, "I love you, Mamie. God bless you, Ociee."

I could not wait to write to Elizabeth. But I had to promise my aunt to keep very quiet about Mr. Lynch's proposal until her decision was made. And I couldn't write to Papa or the boys about it either. I thought I would pop from having to keep the secret. I decided to keep my mind on getting the Murphys' house finished. At least that was one thing we could do to get life back to normal.

After the holidays, I made it my mission to drop by their house on my way home from school every afternoon. I would priss myself up to whatever man who happened to be working outside or on the porch.

"Sir," I'd ask politely, "How much longer do you think it will be before the Murphys' can move back in?"

"Whoever" would tell me he wasn't sure.

I had made my point.

"What's been done today?" I asked another man the next day.

Every day, I'd have another question.

It worked, too. One evening in late January, the man in charge of the Murphy's house, came by to talk with Aunt Mamie. I stayed upstairs doing my homework for school.

At bedtime, she came into my room. "The gentleman said it was no longer necessary for my niece to supervise his men every single day," she related. "However, I am *merely* delivering *his* message," said Aunt Mamie. "I, myself, recommend that you keep on doing just as you have. I think your encouragement is making a difference in the progress they're making." She kissed me on my forehead, " Good for you."

"Thank you, Aunt Mamie."

March was getting close; I resolutely made my daily stops. Mr. Schrader, the friendliest of all the workers, had kindly kept me informed about many of the particulars. Then, late one Thursday afternoon, he hollered to me. My friend said, "I jist want ya to know, today's my last day here."

I poked my head through the window, "Sir?" He replied, "I reckon as your friends will be acomin' back to these parts mightily soon now, little lady."

"Thank YOU, Mr. Schrader!" I raced for home to tell Aunt Mamie the news. Around the corner and down the street I charged. I was grinning so my cheeks were tight and my eyes squinted. I turned up our walk and skipped two steps. My aunt and Mr. Lynch were on the porch. They both leapt to their feet.

"Whatever is it, child?" said Aunt Mamie.

"You won't even believe it! The Murphys' house is all but finished," I was panting. "Mr. Schrader said they'd be home soon, "I said, jumping and waving my arms. "Elizabeth and her folks are coming back where they belong!"

"How wonderful," they echoed.

Aunt Mamie took my hands, and we turned in circles like square dancers. Mr. Lynch clapped as we danced our jig. We could finally celebrate the end of the fire's awful misery. "Victory!" I shouted. "We did it. I did it!"

"Yes, indeed, you did." Aunt Mamie said grabbing the back of her chair. "Whew, happy as I am for all concerned, I must sit down."

"And I'm afraid this is as much excitement as I can take, myself," beamed Mr. Lynch as he bid us good-bye. "I'll see you ladies later."

After he left, we settled down to savor the news. I closed my eyes and smiled. I was pleased Mr. Lynch had been there to hear. Of course, it wasn't unnatural for him to be on our porch. It was ordinary. "Old Horse was resting," so they said. I noticed that Old Horse was needing more rest all the time. I wasn't about to pry, but it seemed to me that Aunt Mamie was enjoying Mr. Lynch's attention. For my part, I hoped she would give him the answer he wanted. Yes, a bunch of good things were coming our way.

In those days, important people came to visit the Vanderbilts. As we lived on Charlotte Street, I often had a chance to watch the goings on. I figured any fine lady who passed by our house *could be* a queen of a foreign country. It followed that every man might be a king. Aunt Mamie told me I was very perceptive, as many of the gentlemen were "Kings of Industry." I didn't know where Industry was, but I did plan to marry a king one day and become Queen of Industry. If I could move by myself to Asheville when I was only nine, I could move almost anywhere once I was grown.

That particular afternoon, we saw a queen. Aunt Mamie started to tap frantically on my shoulder, "Look a there, Ociee, look a there!"

"Look where, Aunt Mamie?" All I saw were ladies riding by on horses.

"Those riders, dear, see the girl in the middle? I saw her picture in the paper. It's Alice Roosevelt, daughter of Theodore Roosevelt, he's the governor of New York, child!" My aunt was talking as fast as a flood. "And he's the famous hero of the Spanish -American War."

They were gone in just seconds, but the event gave Aunt Mamie something to talk about for weeks. I was disappointed that Mr. Roosevelt was just a governor, not a king.

It wasn't too many years later that that we went to see Mr. Roosevelt himself. He still wasn't a king, but he was the President of the United States. I remembered standing out in front of the Battery Park Hotel with Aunt Mamie. We were dressed in our very best clothes, and President Roosevelt was making a speech to the people of Asheville. We didn't see Alice Roosevelt that day. I supposed she was off riding a horse somewhere else.

25

On Friday, Mr. Murphy stopped by to see us on his return trip from the Post Office. He wanted me to know first, before another single living person in Asheville, that Elizabeth and her mother would be arriving home in three weeks. I didn't tell him that I'd already figured it out thanks to Mr. Schrader's disclosure. I hoped Mr. Murphy realized I was the person responsible for hurrying the reconstruction work along. I assumed he did.

He read us the letter. "See ladies, it says right here, 'We're to arrive at the train station at 4 o'clock in the afternoon of March 25'." Elizabeth's father continued, "And here you are, Ociee, your own letter from Elizabeth."

I read mine to myself, it was private. She told me I'd better be there, too. I decided right then to be at the train station by 3 o'clock, or maybe even in the morning, in case the train was really early. Aunt Mamie said she was certain Mr. Lynch would take me.

"For free?" I asked.

"Ociee Nash, listen to you!" she fanned her face with her hand, "I will never take your gumption for granted."

We had invited Mr. Murphy in for a cup of tea to celebrate the wonderful news. We were back in the kitchen when we heard a knock on the front door. Then there came a voice, a familiar voice, not Mr. Lynch's. Not Mr. McCall's. I knew it.

The voice said, "Mamie?"

The voice said, "Ociee? Any Nashes here at home? "

"Papa?" My heart lunged to my neck. "Papa!" My feet were bricks. I couldn't move. I didn't have to. Hearing me shout his name, Papa's feet carried him fast to the kitchen.

"Papa, Papa, oh Papa. You're here! Am I dreaming?"

Papa said not one word. He ran by the ice box, reached out and pulled me up into his strong arms. Papa held me close, as close as when we hugged good-bye all those many months ago in Abbeville. I wouldn't let go of him for fear he'd disappear backwards to Mississippi.

"Ociee," he whispered hardly making a sound.

Aunt Mamie stood back. She watched. Tears rushed down her face.

Papa put me down. My feet touched the tile floor but I felt as if I was floating around the kitchen.

"I guess you're all mighty surprised," laughed Papa.

Aunt Mamie grabbed him and said, "George Nash, you've been surprising me since you were a naughty little boy in knee pants. There's no reason to believe you will change your ways at this late date."

I was grinning so my cheeks squeezed my eyes closed.

My aunt held her arms out high and said, "Now you best be giving your favorite sister a kiss."

Papa did and said, "Mamie, you're my *only* sister, but I'll tell you, girl, I believe you'd be my favorite if I had a hundred more." He motioned for me. We three hung on to one another until Mr. Murphy cleared his throat. He excused himself saying, "I should go and let you enjoy this reunion."

Papa put out his hand and said, "Forgive me, sir, I wasn't thinking of anything but my little girl, here. You must be George Lynch."

"Darling brother, I'd like to introduce Mr. Murphy, this man is Mr. *Murphy*," she insisted.

"Papa, Mr. Murphy is Elizabeth's father. You know all about the Murphys. And Papa, you'll never believe it, but you've come for the best day. Mr. Murphy just told us that Elizabeth is coming home in only three weeks!"

I breathed, "And Papa, you really are here. Will you stay and meet her, will you please?" Then, before he could answer, I blurted out, "Papa, 'course you know that Mr. Lynch asked Aunt Mamie and me to marry him, and she said 'no, no, and no.' I believe that she's just about ready to give in to him. Ask her. Besides, I know you can get her to say she will."

"Gracious sakes alive, Ociee Nash," said Aunt Mamie, "calm yourself, you may just burst like a soap bubble."

"Aunt Mamie, I am bursting, but for happy, not sad."

I wasn't able to sit down for a single second. First, we got the news of Elizabeth and her family. Then Papa, my Papa. There he was standing in the middle of Aunt Mamie's kitchen.

"I am delighted to meet you, Mr. Nash," said Mr. Murphy. "Although, it's more as if I am merely seeing someone I already know. Your little Ociee talks of you frequently. And with enormous affection."

"Mr. Murphy, I talk about Papa and the boys and Mississippi all the time. And I talk about Elizabeth and you and Mrs. Murphy. I suppose that I just about talk all the time," I admitted.

Everyone burst out laughing. I knew why.

"I truly hate to leave this jubilant gathering, but I must run as I have much to do to prepare for my family's reunion," said Mr. Murphy. "Although I cannot think that ours will be quite as extraordinary as this one, it was my great delight to witness yours. I'll see myself to the door. Good day."

He shook hands with Papa again, nodded to my aunt and grinned at me.

"Good day," I teased, "this is the goodest day ever."

"Best day, my dear," Aunt Mamie teased.

"Look how you've grown, my Miss Ociee," said Papa standing back and checking me toe to top. "I can say it out loud now, no letter to mail to say how proud I am of my Ociee. I can shout it out and hug you tight all at the same time. Come here to your Papa."

I was truly going to bust open for joy. "My Papa."

"Well, if I cry any more tears this day, I'll likely drown. Best throw me in the French Broad River and be done with it," said Aunt Mamie. "There's not been a happier vision in this house in years."

"Likely not one since I brought my Bertie home as my bride," said Papa.

"Likely not, George," she replied.

"Papa, before you say another word, please let us know about Ben and Fred," I asked.

"Well, sweet sister, your brothers are missing you. I thought Ben would pack himself in my baggage he was so anxious to come. His teacher invited him to stay in her home while I traveled to surprise you, but he chose to be with Fred instead. I'll tell you more of the story in a while. Can a fellow get a glass of good cold mountain water first?"

"What's this I hear?" said Mr. Lynch as he made his way into the house. "Ed Murphy tells me the fine farmer from Mississippi has come all this way to see who's courting his sister."

"Lands sakes, George Lynch," my aunt blushed up one side and down the other.

I pulled Papa's hand into Mr. Lynch's. "George Nash, please meet George Lynch."

They shook hands.

"See, Papa, two Georges." I liked that. Although it made me feel strange to call Papa, George Nash. I'd be sticking to "Papa" from then on.

Aunt Mamie handed Papa a tall glass of water. Then she said, "I could use some tea. Come, Ociee, help me for a minute. Let's get those menfolk out of our kitchen. Papa and Mr. Lynch went to the parlor and I got out the cups, sugar and cream and our very best silver tray. "Aunt Mamie, isn't it just wonderful, it's just wonderful that Papa is here."

"Yes, dear child, it is, I hope."

"Aunt Mamie?"

26

"It feels good to be in your home, Mamie," said Papa as he drank his tea.

"Our home," she corrected him. "It's mine and yours and now Ociee's."

He had poured the tea into his water glass to let it cool. Papa told my aunt he wasn't much for hot drinks after his morning coffee. As a farmer, he spent more time trying to cool off than trying to get warm.

"That's sweet of you, Mamie, to say *our* home after all these years. Indeed, I am very comfortable here in our childhood home. And, Lord knows how wonderful you have been to my darling Ociee, to welcome her so kindly."

"She's been a joy, she has," smiled my aunt.

The room was still.

"George, even after twenty years of seeing you running your farm, I still remember when you went off to the University of North Carolina. We were all so proud of you. Even though I've visited Mississippi, and seen it for myself, I still don't quite find it natural for you to be working the soil. Restlessness, pioneer yearnings or whatever!"

"Mamie, as always, you are closer to the truth than you know," he said.

"George, what is it?"

"Later, Mamie, later, dear," he said quietly.

His words worried my heart. But I wouldn't allow that worry for long. I was so happy to see Papa. And something told me his answer might bring dark to our day. I wasn't ready. Not just yet. "So, Papa, what do you think about, about," I stammered coming up with something away from the topic to say, "what do you think about Old Horse?"

"Old who? Oh, Mr. Lynch's horse?" Papa said, "Ociee, I imagine you might be more curious about what I think about George Lynch than what I think of his horse. You're talking to your Papa, I know how you work at finding out about things." Papa turned to Mr. Lynch and said, "Fact is, I can't say what I'm thinking right in front of the man."

Aunt Mamie gave me a look like she could have skinned me alive, and her brother, in addition.

Mr. Lynch squirmed in his seat and sort of coughed a mumble sound.

Papa smiled a great big smile, "Ociee, from what I hear from you, and from my dear sister, and from what I see in the man himself, I like him. I know there's no talking your Aunt Mamie into much of anything, but for what it's worth, George has my vote."

Mr. Lynch stood up saying, "It's been a long time since I looked for the approval of a young lady's family." He shook Papa's hand, "Thanks, George." He leaned over and gave my aunt a kiss on her cheek. "Mamie, now you be listening to your brother." Giving me a peck on my forehead, he said, "Ociee, you are a rare one, all right."

"Thank you, Mr. Lynch." I tried to take everything as a compliment.

"I'd like to stay the longer, but I should be about my buggy business," he said. "Besides, you three need your own time." He gave Aunt Mamie another little kiss. She acted miffed. Papa and I thought that was real funny. Mr. Lynch waved good-bye and off he went.

"Old Horse takes me for rides all the time, Papa, and for free. I give him carrots and sugar in return. Mama used to teach me that. She'd say, 'Ociee, mind you now, try to give people treats in return for the kindness they extend to you or yours.'"

Papa said he treasured that. "It seems that you remember a good amount of what your Mama wanted you to learn. Now Aunt Mamie has managed to pick up in her place." He looked

145

toward my aunt, "Thank you, Mamie, you're doing a worthy job with Ociee."

She grinned. "Of course, I am. We both are."

"Papa! Now tell me about my Ben. How big is he? Has he been into mischief?" I was spitting out questions fast as I could. "Tell us some new funny stories about my brother. Oh, Papa, tell us."

"Ociee, Ben is Ben. That's the remarkable truth of it. He's just as you left him, but, for now he's about to survive another year in school. Perhaps I should say his teacher has survived! Now, he's bigger by a good stretch. He's growing like a corn stalk." Papa stood up and with his hand to his chest, he said, "Comes to here on me."

"He's gonna outgrow Fred. I just know it." I yelled, "FRED! Is Fred marrying Rebecca? Will it be soon?" Before he could answer, I announced, "Aunt Mamie and I will travel on the train to the wedding. And we'll decorate the church with beautiful flowers, won't we, Aunt Mamie?"

Papa sank back down on the parlor chair. He looked toward Mamie.

"George, what is it?" she asked.

"Papa?"

He sucked in a mouthful of breath. "It's all tied together," said Papa. "No, Fred is not getting married, not just yet anyway. Ociee, Mamie, listen to me." He sighed. "Our Fred, well, he's gone away. It's all just happened too fast. Fred got a chance to go to work for the railroad and he jumped at it. Always loved the trains, you both know that about him. I didn't have the heart to get in his way. Well, Fred had to report to Tennessee — Memphis, Tennessee — ten days ago. That's where he's being taught his beginning tasks."

Aunt Mamie spoke up, "Good for Fred. I rejoice for him, but I worry for poor little Ben. We know how he misses Ociee so, and now to lose the big brother he worships. Mercy me."

I couldn't open my mouth.

"Well, let me bring to light the rest of the news. At first, Ben kept stomping around like some angry bull. He didn't much know how to talk about his brother without hollering," said Papa. "I didn't know what to do for the boy, mindful I was that he'd already experienced a grown man's lifetime of loss."

"I understand, George," said Aunt Mamie, "Would you please consider sending him here?"

"Oh yes!" I screamed. "That would be grand! There's not nearly so much trouble for him to find in Asheville, and I'll make him behave, Papa."

"*That* would be a wonder, Ociee. And Mamie, once again I find myself grateful to you, but, ladies, now don't get ahead of me just yet," said Papa. "Fred offered to take Ben with him to Memphis so I'd be free to come here for my visit. That Ben couldn't have been more excited if he were going to the other side of the world. I figure he'll tag along with Fred for a time and then, just maybe, he'd be more satisfied at home in Mississippi."

I realized with a start that Papa may be left with no one. There he'd be, no Mama, no Ociee, no Fred, no Ben; he'd be all alone. I said, "Papa, you really do need Ben to help you on our farm now that Fred's gone. I'd best plan to come home as well."

Then came the next blow.

Clearing his throat, Papa said, "The other reason Fred went off is because we've lost our farm."

I burst into tears.

Aunt Mamie sank in her seat.

Papa wanted to explain what had happened. My aunt listened. She nodded her head, her fingers twined around her thumbs. I tried hear him but my ears wouldn't let me. I understood my house was gone, my room was gone. There would be no more sitting with Papa on the porch swing. No more fishing in our pond. No more playing hide and seek in our barn. There'd be no more sprouts in spring for my eyes to find, no more pumpkin seeds to toast in the fall, no more apples or peaches for the train folks.

"Papa, my calf, Rebecca? Where is Rebecca?"

"It grieves me so to tell you, but Rebecca had to be sold with the cows," I sighed. "The chickens, goats, horses, the ducks. They're all sold, dearest. I am sorry, so very, very sorry." Papa's head was in his hands. Aunt Mamie was patting his back.

I cried out. Aunt Mamie got up from Papa and came to hold me. "I named my calf after Fred's Rebecca," I choked out the words, my tears splashed on her dress.

My mouth tasted of salt. I sat there, just a lump of Ociee was all that was left of me. There was no sound except for sniffling.

That night we had our supper in the kitchen. I fixed no flowers for the table. I don't remember what we ate. I don't remember tasting a bite of anything. It wasn't the same kitchen where Papa had walked in and held me tight.

It rained during the night.

The next morning, the sun peeked in my window. It made me think of the dawn after Elizabeth's fire and how it had made things better that morning. But that very same sun couldn't yield enough light to lift my gloom.

I wouldn't let it.

I lay there in my bed for a very long time. Wrapped in Mama's quilt, my cocoon, I wouldn't crawl out, not ever again. I twisted the chain of Mama's locket with my finger. I drew my knees up to my chest and folded my arms in a tight knot.

There was no going back to sleep for me. My head whirled. I was back on the train from Mississippi. The cows and barn and people who flew past the trains window were my people, my barn, my calf.

We Nashes were in a tornado. Ours was a forever tornado which seemed never to stop tearing us apart. We were blown to bits all over my whole world. I was blown to North Carolina. Fred was blown to Tennessee. Papa and Ben were still blowing around in the clouds, goodness knows where they'd ever land.

"Mama, why did you have to die, anyway? That's when things started to go bad for us." I kicked at the covers, freed my arm and shook my finger at her picture. "I hate you for dying on us, Mama. You hear me?"

My lungs sucked in hard. Kicking wild like, I unfurled the quilt and, freeing myself, I jumped from my bed. I glared at myself in the mirror. Wait, what did I just do? No! Mama's locket. It's gone from around my neck. What *did* I do? It can't be lost again. But it was.

I crawled on all fours up and down the baseboard. No locket. With all my strength, I moved the washstand away from the wall. It must have landed behind it. No locket. I pushed my bed away from the wall. Again nothing. I pulled back the curtain. Not there. I quivered at the thought. I must have heaved it out the window when I flung the covers off of me! Was it lost in the trees? In the grass? In the sticky holly bush? Eaten alive in the ivy?

For nearly an hour, I tore apart my room searching, always looking toward the open windows. I just couldn't have done that. Not to myself, not to Mama.

The sun shown in. "Mama, I am so sorry. I don't blame you. Folks don't mean to die. Of all the mamas in Mississippi, I know you wanted most to be alive. I'm not truly mad, Mama. I'm still so sad and so worried, most now for Papa. I'm worried for Ben, for us all."

Plain and simple, I'd let my Ociee temper take me over. All I'd managed to do was lose the one thing I treasured more than anything, more than our farm. I hadn't lost Mama's locket, worse. I had thrown it away.

"Forgive me, Mama." I couldn't look directly at her picture as I said the words. I couldn't let my eyes catch her gaze. I feared her smile was gone.

My heart was torn in big awful chunks, but I had to dress. I'd have to go downstairs and tell Papa and Aunt Mamie what I'd done. Maybe we could all three look outside. Maybe. I felt as if I'd been on a huge swing since the day before. First, I was flying high, free as a bird, Papa had come. Then down toward earth I'd spun with the terrible bad news. I wanted to fly up again but, CRASH, into a tree, the huge swing had hurled me. It hurled me the very same way I must have hurled the locket. My life was a mess that morning.

I brushed my hair and started to put on my socks. How could I be so happy to see Papa only hours ago and then, the very next morning manage to lose my most valuable possession. Papa lost our farm; I lost our locket.

The sun shone higher. Suddenly, out of the corner of my eye, I glimpsed a flicker. Almost afraid to look any closer, I forced myself. There was a glimmer. The sun highlighted a shining surface. Was it a dew drop? An imagined sparkle? A beetle bug, maybe. I slowly walked toward the glow.

Mama's locket.

"Thank you, sunshine."

"Thank you, Mama."

"Yes, Mama, no more Ociee tempers, I promise."

I squeezed the broken link back together and kissing the tiny heart, I fastened it around my neck. I finished dressing and started downstairs. That locket, once again, was to give me my courage back. I could hear the voices of Papa and Aunt Mamie from the kitchen.

27

"I meant what I said, George," said my aunt. "I never did think of you as a farmer. I'm afraid you are more of an idealist. You're a kind man, brother dear, with a heart far too big for his pocketbook and dreams even bigger. And, you are, most certainly, a better accountant than you are a man of the soil. I'm sorry, but you asked for my thoughts on this."

I stopped in the hall to listen. I knew that wasn't right on my part, but I had to hear what Aunt Mamie and Papa were saying. I scrunched down by the hall tree.

Papa replied, "Mamie, you know me all too well. I was dedicated to the idea of working our land. My commitment wasn't the problem." He laughed, "I just wasn't much good at farming." Papa had a way of laughing to cover up his gloom.

His voice got serious again, "What hurts me so is that we, Bertie and I, put so many years, so much of our sweat into that land. The biggest part of our souls rests there on our place. Mamie, until this time in my life, I had always assumed that I could and would accomplish pretty much anything I set out to do."

I listened as Aunt Mamie pushed her chair back. She walked away from the table toward the window by the sink. She commented, "I understand how terribly disappointed you are, George. But you must remember that you are not an old man as yet. And I have known your wife most of her precious life. She wouldn't want to see you rebuking yourself this way. She'd want you to stand tall and go on in the pursuit of new dreams."

I heard Papa sigh.

She poured his coffee and continued, "You know George, you talked about how determined you are. I surely see a great deal of *you* in Ociee. Why, she might well be the joyfulness of Bertie with the confidence and fire of her dear father. "

I almost jumped from behind the door. Truth was, I liked hearing her say that. But, for once, I kept still.

"Thank you for saying that, Mamie, but I hope Ociee has a larger measure of her Mama in her. If I'd still had the strength of my dear Bertie, I believe I'd have saved our farm."

"Now, George, listen here. Let's look for the good in this. Maybe that farm shackled you to the land. Look at Fred. He can now be off doing what he's always wanted to do. He's been talking train talk from his first breath," she said. "And Ben. Perhaps moving to Abbeville and making a fresh start is the right step for that darling boy to take. But, brother of mine, don't you forget, I do dearly wish you would send Ben to us."

"Mamie, I can't do it. I need one of my children at my side. And Ben seems to be the one who most needs a papa. Dear sister, you've shed needed light on this for me. I think it best to take Homer Fitch up on his offer."

"I think you should, George, for every reason we discussed," Aunt Mamie said.

That was more than I could contain. Into the kitchen I burst, "What?"

Papa turned over his coffee.

"And good morning to you, Ociee," said Aunt Mamie. "Been outside that door a good long time, have you?"

She and Papa laughed.

I was embarrassed.

"Who shot that girl out of a cannon?" asked Papa as he sopped up his spilled coffee.

"I'm sorry everyone, I just, well, Papa, are you gonna work at Fitch's? Are you moving to Abbeville?"

"Can't keep much from your sweet ears, can we, Ociee! Come sit in my lap."

"Papa, I'm too big for that."

"Not until after your next birthday, said Papa. "Here, sit. Now, Miss Ociee, I am thinking about living in Abbeville. Your

Aunt Mamie seems to like the idea," he said smiling at his sister. Fitch's Mercantile has expanded a good many ways in the last year. Ociee, you may not recognize the place. Mr. Fitch has the latest farm implements; and he's built on his own cotton gin, and a new grist mill. With all his improvements, Mr. Fitch approached me with an offer to manage things for him. We've been friends for years, and we trust one another."

Aunt Mamie said proudly, "Mr. Fitch is well aware that your Papa is very intelligent and an excellent bookkeeper to boot." She patted him as she got up to start cooking breakfast.

I crawled from Papa's lap to the chair. Looking at Papa and then Aunt Mamie, I said, "I wish we still had Mama and our farm, and that Fred was at home, and that things were like they used to be."

"I do, too, Miss Ociee," said Papa, "I wish that with all my heart."

"Papa!" I screamed and bolted out of the kitchen.

"Ociee, wait! Mamie, what in this world?"

Aunt Mamie said, "I guess we're about to find out."

I was back in a jiffy, and in my hand was Mama's picture. "Look, Papa, I wrote you about it. Now have a look for yourself." I gave him the gypsy's painting.

Papa said not a word.

"What do you think, Papa? Isn't it a lovely image of Mama. Isn't she beautiful?"

Papa kept staring at it.

"Papa?"

"I, I don't know what to say," said Papa as he reached for his handkerchief. He wiped his eyes.

"Papa, please say it looks like Mama. Is it your Bertie, you know, the prettiest girl in Marshall County?" I was so afraid he didn't like the painting. I was thinking that, just maybe, it didn't look a thing like Mama.

Aunt Mamie spoke, "George, tell us what you think."

"Ociee, Mamie, this takes my speech away. Why, it is a wonder! I am truly grateful, and I am touched deeply that my daughter has such a treasure. I wish I could thank your gypsy man."

"Papa, I don't think he's the thanking kind. But he surely knows he made me happy. I think I was enthusiastic enough for every one of us."

"I imagine you were, Ociee; somehow I can almost see how you must have reacted to seeing your mother's dear face. Look how she smiles. Please look at that! Mamie, isn't it a marvel?"

"Your daughter has waited many months to show this portrait to you, George. Looks as if it were worth the wait."

Papa smiled.

The bacon was sizzling. Aunt Mamie cracked the eggs.

Papa said he could look at the painting all day, but he felt he needed to share his thoughts while they were fresh. He said, "At this point my plan would call for Ben to join me before school starts and, once we get settled, you Ociee can think about coming home as well. There is a nice little house close to Ben's school and to Fitch's. Fred will come from time to time, and soon, I imagine, Rebecca will be in our family also. Dearest, that's the reason I wanted to see you. I couldn't simply write a letter about all of this. I had to be here with you."

"Coming home?" I half asked, half accepted. Where was home? Home was first our farm. Home was then my house on Charlotte Street. Home was with Aunt Mamie? Home was with Papa and Ben? Fred? Rebecca?

"Perhaps, Mamie will want to travel out with you," suggested Papa. "That is if she's not too busy riding buggies," he teased.

"I declare, George, will you ever stop picking on me?" My aunt popped the back of Papa's head, "Buggies or no buggies, I intend to remain in Asheville; there will be no frontier living for this city girl."

"City girl," I thought to myself, if I were to live with Papa and Ben, I'd be an Abbeville girl, like Fred's Rebecca. "Tell you one thing," I stated, standing up as tall as I could, "I am just proud as I can be that I am a little of both. I am a city girl that knows all about being a farm girl."

Papa stood up and clapped for me. I clapped for him. He and Aunt Mamie gave me a hug. I hugged them back.

We three sat down for breakfast. After Papa blessed the food, I announced, "I am one hungry almost-grown young lady, a citified farm girl who likes her breakfast. Please pass the biscuits!"

About five minutes into breakfast, which meant Papa and I were nearly done, Mr. Lynch came by for me. With all the excitement, I almost forgot. Here it was our day to go for the mail together. I usually got all excited about getting a letter from Papa. Today was different. Papa had delivered himself.

Mr. Lynch joined us for his coffee time and we tried to tell him everything that had happened. All he could reply was, "Whew."

He did ask my aunt if she was a part of any of this moving business.

Aunt Mamie said, "Don't worry for one minute, George Lynch. I have my niche carved out just like I want right here in Asheville at 66 Charlotte Street."

Mr. Lynch puffed up and said, "Mamie! Does that mean you are finally saying yes to me?"

Papa and I looked up, our mouths open.

"George Lynch, not just yet. You are one persistent suitor, I declare."

Mr. Lynch smiled at Papa and said, "Does stubborn run in the family?"

"The whole family, George, the whole headstrong group of us."

155

Papa offered to stay home with my aunt and wash up the dishes. I washed my teeth and got ready for our mail trip. I greeted Old Horse, promised him a treat for later in the day and jumped on Mr. Lynch's buggy.

"Isn't my Papa the handsomest man?" I asked as Mr. Lynch drove the buggy to the Post Office.

"Can't say I noticed the handsomeness of him. I did think him a fine man and that had not a thing to do with how much you and Mamie love him. I am glad he's not taking you two away back to Mississippi with him. Ociee, he's not come to fetch you, has he?"

I shrugged my shoulders in response.

28

Putting aside any seriousness, we rode on to the Post Office for our mail. The postmaster greeted us and began to gather up everything.

"Any news up your way?" asked Mr. Hightower.

"My Papa came to see me, all the way from Mississippi," I proudly announced. "Of course, he came to see Aunt Mamie, too. And to meet Mr. Lynch," I giggled.

Mr. Lynch shuffled from one foot to the other.

Mr. Hightower smiled, "All the way from Mississippi, you say?"

I explained that Papa, I called him George Nash, had grown up in Asheville and needed a taste of his old hometown. "And, as much as Papa missed me, he also wanted to see what he thought of his sister's *gentleman caller*."

Mr. Lynch quickly turned me around, thanked Mr. Hightower for our mail, and said we must be on our way.

Back up in the wagon, he explained, "Ociee, telling Mr. Hightower anything serves to tell all of Asheville." He clicked his tongue and Old Horse started for home. He said, "Everybody for blocks around, who isn't already aware of our business, will be brought up to date by dark."

"Good," I thought, but I didn't say it. I just smiled shyly.

I looked through the mail. There was a letter for Mr. Lynch which he slid in his pocket. We also had a parcel for Aunt Mamie, likely the buttons we ordered all the way from New York. Most special of all, I got a letter. It was from Ben.

"Oh, Mr. Lynch, will you please slow Old Horse so I can read this right away? I surely cannot wait until home. You know that buggy riding and reading makes me upchuck."

"Ociee, I know that all too well. For such an amazing event as getting a letter from your brother, I will gladly pull to the side of the road. Maybe Mr. Hightower will look out and see us and get his curiosity churned up for the second time this morning!"

I was too anxious to open my letter to wonder about such things as the postmaster's curiosity. Besides, I liked to hear him tell about folks, I learned many interesting things from Mr. Hightower.

Ociee dear,

How did you like that, Ociee dear, instead of Dear Ociee? Miss Brown showed me that. Anyway, I am in Memphis with Fred. He is at his railroad job. He says he'll soon be <u>driving</u> those big engines instead of feeding the coal into them. Fred's being cocky, and I think he's happy.

Guess what? I got to ride on the train just like you. Here's what. I don't think I'm going to be a telegraph operator anymore. On the train trip to Memphis, I decided that since Fred is going to be the railroad man, I may join the circus. Remember that bear we saw in Holly Springs? Well, I think I may train a whole group of bears, but mean ones, bears with giant teeth. My bears would growl all the time.

How are you? I liked your letter about the snow. I liked your letter about Elizabeth's fire even more. When did you get so brave, Ociee? How tall are you?

Miss Brown is making me read books. But guess what? She gave me a book to read about cowboys and guns and buffaloes. I may go out to California now that I have been to Memphis. Do you think the ocean out there could be much bigger that the Mississippi River? I can't see how it could be.

Ociee, are you coming home?

Papa can't farm without me and Fred, so we are moving to Abbeville. At first, I was sad, kind of like you were when you had to leave to go help out Aunt Mamie. Then I figured it would be too hard for just me to run our farm with only Papa. Oh well, now I can decide between the going out West and my bear act with the circus.

Papa says I will have to go to school until I am at least fourteen-years old! That is forever away, seems to me.

Papa must be there visiting you now. I wish I could have come, but Fred needed me, too. He promised he'd take me to the dock to see a showboat coming in on Friday. I can't wait. I will write you about that in my next letter.

This was a good letter, wasn't it, Ociee? Please let Papa and Aunt Mamie read it, because my hand is too tired of writing to write another.

If you don't come home with Papa, do you want to join the circus with me? You could be a juggler. I'll help you.

Ben, Bear Trainer or Cowboy

Once back at the house, Mr. Lynch tied up his horse and buggy and held open our front door for me. Papa and Aunt Mamie were still back in the kitchen. "Mailman and mail-lady," I shouted. "Something's for you, Aunt Mamie, and for me, too!" I produced Ben's letter. Aunt Mamie put her package aside as I read it out loud to everyone.

I will never figure out what was so funny about Ben's letter, but both Papa and Aunt Mamie were holding their stomachs laughing at it. Mr. Lynch watched us as if we were a comedy troupe. Oh well, I thought it was interesting and surely the longest letter Ben ever wrote to anyone. I would put it for keeps in my candy box.

Much to my surprise, while we were gone to the Post Office, Aunt Mamie and Papa fixed us a picnic lunch. They had planned for us to take a nice long walk to the park. However, once Mr. Lynch spotted the basket and, more importantly, smelled the goodies hidden inside, he said his hunger got the best of him. In a flick of a puppy's tail, all four of us were touring around Asheville courtesy of Old Horse. Mr. Lynch said, "Nothing wrong with taking a day off when a man wants to be with *his* family."

159

Aunt Mamie teased, "That man will do anything for some of my good cooking."

I didn't much care, I just knew I was riding in the buggy up front with Mr. Lynch and all I had to do to see my Papa was turn around and look. He and my aunt started looking about at all the changes in Asheville since he and Mama had gone west. Papa was astounded.

"Ociee, when your Mama and I left for Mississippi, Asheville was not more than a town, why, it's grown up just like my children. I feel like I'm lost in the dust."

Mr. Lynch told us Asheville had gone from just over 2,500 people to nearly 15,000 in the last decade. They started to discuss railroads, the new cotton mill, and folks coming to the mountains for their health. I just loved listening to all my most favorite grown people talking amongst themselves. While they mentioned the spectacular Battery Park Hotel, or the new government building at Patton Avenue and Haywood, or the soon-to- be-built medical building, I was more absorbed in the high-spirited sounds of their voices and the beat of Old Horse's hoofs on the street beneath our buggy.

When Papa made mention of the newly-lighted downtown or the streetcars and motor cars, Mr. Lynch complained. "That'll be the death of me, I'll tell you, George," he snarled. "Oh, those carbon lights are fine enough, but the motored demons scare my horse!"

Aunt Mamie chimed in, "Now George, that's modern, don't you know?"

"Old Horse hates the noise, that's what I know, Mamie, my dear."

"Yes, dear," she replied.

Papa's eyes and mine met. His eyebrows wiggled.

Aunt Mamie continued to point out the new buildings, streetlights, impressive churches, streetcars, schools, and elegant houses. Papa just shook his head. "My Heavens above," he'd repeat over and over again.

I explained to him I had been dumbfounded when I first arrived, too. "Papa," I said, "You'll get accustomed to it. Soon it will seem like Asheville's always been this way. You'll see."

What I most valued about our outing that day was the feeling of joy I had within myself. I relished the unqualified contentment of riding in Mr. Lynch's whole buggy full of Nashes.

I thought back to our Christmas tour of town, or "city" as Papa was insisting to say. I remembered missing my Papa so desperately on our holiday ride. Less than three months later, there I was, I had Papa with me along with my darling aunt and her gentleman caller. The sadness lifted like a velvet curtain on the stage.

The whole next week was like that. We stayed busy having fun and doing interesting things. Aunt Mamie said she didn't get a thing done for her customers. "Ociee, my darling child, this one time it is perfectly all right," she explained. "It is our opportunity to build memories, and we must take advantage of such moments."

Thursday, we got dressed in our Sunday best and went to eat in the main dining room of the Battery Park. I recalled one of my dreams, wasn't it to be a queen? I surely felt like royalty that night.

Another thing we did involved the Vanderbilts. At least, I liked to think Mr. Vanderbilt picked that particular time to open his gardens for a special reason. I thought it was because he heard Mr. Nash wanted to see them.

We decided to go on Sunday. Papa called for a different buggy so Mr. Lynch could relax and enjoy our excursion. Our family got all gussied up and, along with a good number of other curious Asheville people, we drove to the Biltmore Estate.

Mr. Lynch didn't say a critical word about the driver, but I determined he was a slowpoke. Aunt Mamie told me to "shush up" and declared I was spoiled by Mr. Lynch and Old Horse. As we rode through the Biltmore's front gates, I sat up extra straight. Papa, Aunt Mamie, Mr. Lynch and I were most certainly fancy folks that afternoon. Indeed, we were.

161

At first, we couldn't make a sound short of a swoon. We rolled through the Biltmore's rolling wooded grounds. Our necks twisting, we pointed and punched one another with sounds of, "Oweee, and look 'a there, and glory be!"

I felt as if I were plopped right over there in France or someplace with a real castle and land tended by the royal gardeners. I finally said, "I wouldn't be one bit surprised if Sir Lancelot himself were to gallop out from behind that fir tree."

I gazed at the rivers of ferns and foliage that danced throughout trees, trees that seemed to flow on into forever, trees that touched the sky and allowed in only flickers of blue sky and sunlight. As we trotted in and out of open spaces, we discovered groupings of circles and curves of early Spring flowers every color in a rainbow.

I imagined that my aunt's whole brightly-wallpapered house had burst to life and multiplied one thousand times. I was a teeny tiny fairy flitting about to see each bloom, every leaf. If I were to fly forever, I could never see it all.

I made a decision right then and there. "Papa," I announced, "One of these days, I'll live in a garden with flowers and trees and bushes and birds and chipmunks. And you can come and live there, too!"

"Ociee, wherever do you get such outlandish notions?" he asked.

Aunt Mamie cleared her throat really loudly, "I expect you know, George Nash. She's a later edition of her papa! And best she keep nourishing those notions, for that's the food that will give her dreams life."

"You pegged me again, Mamie," said Papa. As usual, I didn't try to figure what their conversation was all about. I assumed it was what big brothers and big sisters do. Their talking was akin to Fred's or Ben's with me, but with full-grown words.

"Perhaps, dear George, you could benefit from your daughter's gift of enthusiasm," she finished.

Papa nodded.

As we rode out through the Biltmore's gate, he said, "Ociee, I'll need your help tomorrow."

"You'll surely have it, Papa."

29

Just after breakfast the next morning, Papa wanted me to take him to the telegraph office. I knew exactly where to show him to go, because it was the first place I ever went in Asheville. It was where I sent my telegram to Papa and my brothers when I got off the train.

As we went in, I stopped Papa and admitted to him, "I've got to tell you now, Papa, I was so scared when I sent you that wire. I didn't let on, but when Aunt Mamie wasn't there to greet me, I just knew she'd changed her mind about wanting me to come. I near about wanted to turn and walk all the way back to Abbeville."

"My poor darling daughter," Papa squeezed my hand, "I was so upset when Mamie wrote me about what had happened. My heart sank whenever I thought of you looking into all those strange faces who didn't know who my little girl was."

"It was terrible, Papa."

"I know, but I was both proud and amazed at your courage and smartness, Ociee. Dearest, when I read your telegram, you acted as if not one thing had gone wrong. I had no idea."

"Well, I sent it to you *hoping and praying* I was right about being fine!" I replied.

Papa hugged me. I felt as safe in his arms as I had felt all alone that frightful September afternoon.

Papa had made his decision the day before. He penned his telegram accepting Mr. Fitch's offer, and we both watched as the operator tapped it to Abbeville. I think he was the same man who sent my message to Papa. I know he wore the same hat, that hat and his hair I remembered. I kept traveling my mind back to September and feeling mighty glad the springtime had finally come to Asheville.

On our way home, Papa stopped and gave me another big hug. He said sort of chuckling, "Do you remember wiring us about a monkey?"

"Surely do, Papa, that was mostly for Ben to enjoy," I said.

"He talked of nothing else for weeks," laughed Papa. "By the time Ben told that story around our community, the tiny monkey was a gorilla and his little sister fought him *something fierce.*"

"I should have guessed he'd tell a yarn like that!"

We walked all the way home laughing and talking. That felt fine to me. I loved for our neighbors to wave at me while I walked with my Papa. I was proud when Papa waved back at them.

In one short day, Mr. Fitch wired back. The telegram was delivered to our house. It read:

Fine decision George STOP
You'll not regret STOP
Come immediately STOP
Homer Fitch STOP

The *good news* was shaded in sorrow.

The *good news* would end Papa's visit.

He talked to me in the kitchen, "Ociee, I hate to leave, I know it hurts you, because it hurts me so. I can tell you we would both feel this pain in our hearts tomorrow or next month just as much as we would today. Putting off doesn't soften the good-bye. I just wish I could divide myself in three selves: one Papa for Ociee, one Papa for Ben and one Papa for Fred."

"Four selves, Papa, one for Mr. Fitch," I poked out my lip angrily as I said Mr. Fitch.

Papa shook his head and smiled, knowing I was needing to fuss about things.

"Five selves," I spoke up again, "Aunt Mamie needs one self to be her brother."

"Land sakes, Ociee," Aunt Mamie retorted. She had come in while we were talking. Putting her hands on Papa's shoulders, she said, "My brother is my brother whether he's in Asheville or Abbeville. He's likely to turn up anytime. Makes life more interesting, don't you know?"

"I s'pose you're right, I just like things better when I can see him up close," I argued.

She told me to take a good long look at Papa sitting there in the kitchen chair. "Now, quick, close your eyes real tight. You'll capture an image. Trust me on this. Next week, should you be lonesome for him, you can stand in this special spot, close your eyes again, open them fast and there he'll be! I promise you'll have a glimpse."

"*Really*, Aunt Mamie?" I asked.

"It has worked for me for years," she said as she held out her hands, palms up and raised her shoulders.

Mr. Lynch came by in the early morning two days later. We were almost ready to go. At least, Papa was packed, and we had gotten dressed. Our hearts were still working mightily on being ready for yet another farewell.

Thank gracious goodness Aunt Mamie had taught me how to *capture Papa's image*. I'd spent hours trying to do just that in every spot I could think of from one end of our house to the other. Mostly, I was capturing Papa's laugh because I looked so silly squnching my eyes so purposefully. Actually, my lids *were* fairly sore from my efforts.

Mr. Lynch drove us to the train station. It certainly wasn't the happy buggy ride of the past few weeks. However, I was getting accustomed to folks departing. And, at the very least, I was beginning to realize that good-byes tend eventually to become hellos.

At the train station, Papa shook Mr. Lynch's hand, "Thanks, George," he said. "Keep looking after my girls for me."

"My pleasure," said Mr. Lynch.

Then Papa hugged his sister. "I'll never be able to say how much I appreciate your loving us, especially my Ociee, here," said Papa.

"*Our* Ociee," corrected Aunt Mamie.

Papa smiled. "And I had such a wonderful visit. Simply being home was what the doctor ordered for this Nash. Still can't drink in all the growth around town, but one thing stays the same. You, my dear sister. I thank you and I love you." With that he kissed her.

Aunt Mamie bawled buckets. Mr. Lynch had to go to her.

Next Papa scooped me up. "Whew, heavier than when I came!"

"All those picnics, I reckon," I tried to giggle, but the lump was growing. Aunt Mamie's crying had set me off.

"Ociee, you keep being a big girl, I am forever proud of you," boasted Papa.

"I will," I promised.

The train pulled into the station.

It wasn't nearly long enough before the "All Aboard" sounded. My stomach dropped. My eyes welled up.

I saw how hard it was to be the person staying, the person who had to wave good-bye and stay put. Papa kissed me last and said, "I love you." He walked up the train's steps. Turning he shouted, "*I will see you soon.*" The roar of the engine couldn't keep me from hearing the last sounds of my Papa. "*I love you, my Ociee.*"

Papa went to his seat and poked his head out the window. We could hardly see him for the black smoke.

"George, don't you be falling out," hollered my aunt.

"What's that?" he shouted.

"I love you, Papa!" I knew he heard me.

Aunt Mamie allowed me to run beside the train for just seconds. I yelled, "Papa! I'm glad you came! Hey to Ben and Fred and Mr. Fitch *and* Abbeville Rebecca! I love you, Papa. Bye, Papa, Papa, Papa."

The train was gone.

Mr. Lynch put his arms around both us girls and we left the station. The familiar emptiness was there. We rode toward home quietly.

When we passed Elizabeth's rebuilt house, Mr. Murphy was standing out front. He waved as Mr. Lynch slowed Old Horse, "Two weeks and counting, Ociee," he beamed.

My heart filled up.

"I'll be counting the minutes now, Mr. Murphy."

That night I sat alone on the front porch staring at the spot where Papa had sat hours before. It was true, I could blink, and his face would appear for a second. It was his touch my eyes couldn't capture.

I thought about going back to Abbeville come the next school year, but I couldn't decide for certain. Not just then. Ben might still find his way to Charlotte Street. I smiled and wondered if Asheville was ready for the mischief from a boy like my brother.

Fred could well decide to buy his own railroad company and become a wealthy man like Mr. Vanderbilt. I wasn't a bit anxious about him. Perhaps he would come for a visit, too, and bring Rebecca, *his soon-to-be new wife*. I squirmed some at that notion. Anyhow they would have to come because Aunt Mamie wanted to meet Rebecca, and Mr. Lynch wanted to meet everyone who had something to do with my aunt. Gracious, I wondered if Aunt Mamie herself might decide to be the next bride in our family.

My mind was flitting like a firefly from one thought to the next. I was feeling better about Papa, because Papa was feeling better. Aunt Mamie told me so. She said, "Don't you worry about your Papa and his sorrowful things. He is healing about the farm, and maybe his misery over Bertie is softening in some small way, as well."

She also assured me things would work out exactly like they were supposed to about Papa's new work. I wasn't troubled over that because I figured that my Papa was smart. If he didn't like Fitch's, he'd just decide to run for President of the United States.

Folks never knew what us Nashes were going to do or even where we might turn up next. To us, home became the spot where we made our nest. It was *who nested* that mattered most.

In our old nest, I had pictured Papa as an eagle and Mama as a wren; Ben, a jaybird, of course. Season to season brings changes. Fred was growing to be a Canadian goose. And me? That evening on Aunt Mamie's porch, I saw myself as one of her chirpy, cheery yellow canary birds. But, who knew, I might choose instead to be an eager little owl anxious for wisdom.

I thought of my new nest: Aunt Mamie, already a fine plump hen; Mr. Lynch, a rooster; and in the months to come, Fred's nest might include Rebecca, a silly duck!

I pushed Mama's locket into the soft place on my neck and called inside to my aunt. She came out and joined me. I reminded her that we had forgotten one of our projects, "We've yet to come up with that name for our house, remember, Aunt Mamie?"

She smiled, "Indeed, we must do that! What's your thought, Ociee?"

"How do you like *Nash Nest*?" I asked.

"Lovely! There will not be another with such an interesting name," she said. "*Nash Nest*, it is."

I couldn't wait to share the news with Elizabeth. We would have to come up with a grand name for her home. I expected that to be among our first matters to work on together.

Aunt Mamie looked over at me and said, "*Nash Nest*, Ociee, you are such a clever girl, how blessed I am to have you here."

"Me, too, Aunt Mamie. I am truly happy you have me, too."

"Dear, what would you think if Mr. Lynch joined us in our nest? Well, not just yet, maybe, but one of these days?"

"Oh Aunt Mamie, that's dandy with me!" I said. "But please don't be waiting for too many 'one of these days.'"

Aunt Mamie patted my knee.

"If Mr. Lynch was a bird, what kind would he be?" I asked my aunt.

"You do ask some of the most unusual questions, I declare! Let's see. A robin? No, delightful, but small for George. How about a puffy chested dove? That's not quite it either. I'll dare to say you already have something in mind?"

"Yes, Aunt Mamie, I do. Mr. Lynch would almost have to be a fine red rooster!"

With that, we two cock-a-doodle-dooed until we laughed hysterically. A passerby looked and picked up his pace. We laughed all the harder.

And then we were quiet.

As we sat together, a little robin perched on our porch's rail. A moment later, she was gone.